RIP VAN WINKLE

And

THE LEGEND OF SLEEPY HOLLOW

WASHINGTON IRVING

TWO TALES

RIP VAN WINKLE.

and

THE LEGEND OF

SLEEPY HOLLOW.

Illustrated by Barry Moser
With an Introduction by Alexander Eliot

Harcourt Brace Jovanovich, Publishers
San Diego   New York   London

Requests for permission to make copies of any part of the work should be mailed to: Permissions, Harcourt Brace Jovanovich, Publishers, Orlando, Florida 32887.

Library of Congress Cataloging-in-Publication Data
Irving, Washington, 1783-1859.
  Two tales.
  Previously published under title: Rip Van Winkle and The legend of Sleepy Hollow. West Hatfield, Mass. : Pennyroyal Editions, 1984.
  Summary: These two most popular of Irving's tales are presented as first published in 1819-20.
  [1. New York (State)—Fiction. 2. Short stories]
I. Irving, Washington, 1783-1859. Legend of Sleepy Hollow. 1986. II. Moser, Barry, ill. III. Title.
PS2068.A1   1986   813′.2 [Fic]   86-12109
ISBN 0-15-192280-2

Printed in the United States of America
First edition
A B C D E

LIST OF ILLUSTRATIONS

Rip Van Winkle

The Legend of Sleepy Hollow

INTRODUCTION

"I was always fond of visiting new scenes, and observing strange characters and manners," Washington Irving once remarked. "Even when a mere child I began my travels, and made many tours into foreign parts and unknown regions of my native city, to the frequent alarm of my parents, and emolument of the town-crier. As I grew into boyhood, I extended the range of my observations. My holiday afternoons were spent in rambles about the surrounding country. I made myself familiar with all its places famous in history or fable. I knew every spot where a murder or robbery had been committed, or a ghost seen. I visited the neighboring villages and added greatly to my stock of knowledge by noting their habits and customs, and conversing with their sages and great men. I even journeyed one long summer's day to the summit of the most distant hill, whence I stretched my eye over many a mile of *terra incognita*, and was astonished to find how vast a globe I inhabited."

Doesn't Irving the boy resemble his own Rip Van Winkle in character? Rip loved wandering the wilds with his faithful hound and fowling-piece, or sitting slouched on the bench before the village inn, "telling endless sleepy stories about nothing." Some affinity is to be expected between an author and his most famous creation. Rip's long, long sleep amounted to a little death; his very name suggests the intitials for "Rest in Peace." Yet he eventually awoke to a new world where, after all, things went on as before only better.

Something similar occurred in Irving's own career. Born in New York in 1783 (the year when the Treaty of Paris capped the triumph of our Revolution), Irving was the eleventh child in a strict, Scots Covenanter merchant clan. New York was then an agricultural and port community of only 23,000, mostly clustered down around the Battery. Not exactly rebellious but amiably undisciplined and often unwell, Irving dreamed his way through law school. In the sleepy town of his youth, he afterwards averred, "the very words learning, education, taste and talents were unheard of; a bright genius was an animal unknown and a bluestocking lady would have been regarded with as much wonder as a horned frog or a fiery dragon."

In 1800, Irving made his first 150-mile voyage up the Hudson to Albany, soaking in Dutch and Indian lore along the way. Returning, he took up journalism, in desultory style, as relaxation from his half-hearted law-office work. He had a sweetheart: Matilda Hoffman, the daughter of the lawyer in whose office Irving was employed. At eighteen, she died, and something in the youth was forever crushed. Irving aged overnight. Hoping to restore his good cheer, Irving's prospering elder brothers packed him off across the Atlantic for a Grand Tour of the continent.

On that first trip to Europe, Irving met the celebrated blue-stocking Madame de Staël, the sculptor Antonio Canova, the naturalist Baron von Humboldt, and last but not least the most promising American painter then on the loose: Washington Alston. Plainly the whole experience "took." Like Rip, Irving woke up. The Old World seemed so much greater, more advanced and more lively as well, than he had ever dared to imagine.

Soon after his return to New York, Irving's literary genius bloomed. He was eventually to make his home abroad, finding good friends and admirers everywhere. Among them were Sir Walter Scott and Lord Byron. The reading public at the time regarded Irving as the peer of such great men. William Makepeace Thackeray dubbed him "The first Ambassador whom the New World of Letters sent to the Old." And for almost a century thereafter, Irving's tales were employed as first-readers for students of English the world over.

"It has been a matter of marvel to my European readers," Irving himself remarked with gentle complacency, "that a man from the wilds of America should express himself in tolerable English. I was looked upon as something new and strange in literature, a kind of demi-savage with a feather in his hand instead of on his head."

Irving passed most of his middle years in England and Spain. At age fifty, he returned to settle down in a rambling cottage within strolling distance of Sleepy Hollow itself, not far up the Hudson from New York. "Sunnyside," as he called the place, boasted a host of chimneys and old-Dutch-style, crow-stepped gables, plus deep shady porches festooned with honeysuckle and trumpet-creepers. The house became a Mecca for literary pilgrims, where the genial bachelor held forth with mild grace.

Edgar Allan Poe was Irving's opposite in temperament. Yet Poe in fairness named him "the most deservedly eminent among all the pioneers of American literature."

If that doesn't mean much to us today, the reason is clear. Irving himself explained what would have to happen in a whimsical essay on "The Mutability of Literature." This tour-de-force features a debate between himself and a disgruntled book residing in the library of Westminster Abbey, London.

"What a plague do they mean," the cobwebby quarto grumbles to the author, "by keeping several thousand volumes of us shut up here, and watched by a set of old vergers, like so many beauties in a harem, merely to be looked at now and then by the dean? Books were written to give pleasure and to be enjoyed; and I would have a rule passed that the dean should pay each of us a visit at least once a year; or if he is not equal to the task, let them once in a while turn loose the whole school of Westminster among us, that at any rate we may have an airing."

In his essay Irving replies at length. "The stream of literature," he ruefully informs the lonely little book, "has swelled into a torrent–augmented into a river–expanded into a sea. A few centuries since, five or six hundred manuscripts constituted a great library; but what would you say to libraries such as actually exist, containing three or four hundred thousand volumes; legions of authors at the same time busy; and the press going on with fearfully unceasing activity, to double and quadruple the number? I tremble for posterity . . . The world will inevitably be overstocked with good books. It will soon become the employment of a lifetime merely to learn their names. Many a man of passable information, at the present day, reads scarcely anything but reviews; and before long a man of erudition will be little better than a mere walking catalogue."

He was so right about all that. In the upshot, Irving's own immensely distinguished twenty-volume life-work is largely ignored today. Two of his tales, however, survive as an enchanted islet in the vast, tumultuous ocean of literature.

Schoolchildren in particular come skipping ashore here. So do many adults as well, for pure love of Irving's sorcery. These stories intermingle the sound of far-bowled thunder with the sight of "odd-looking personages playing at nine-pins." They contrast the jolly tinkle of tankards to the persistent thrum of pursuing hooves. They set the screaming and chattering of a blue-jay, "in his gay light blue coat and white underclothes," against the "drowsy undertone with which men talk in the dark."

"Rip Van Winkle" and "The Legend of Sleepy Hollow" alike recast immortal, worldwide myths so craftily as to recall the Dutch pewter, Indian feather-work and cloak-of-Joseph quilts peculiar to young America. These stories cast a roseate Hudson River haze of all-transforming mystery athwart our nation's springtime years.

Washington Irving died in 1859, at home at "Sunnyside." On the day of his funeral, New York City's courts all adjourned, the flags fell to half-mast, and the bells of the whole town tolled for him. Amongst Irving's personal effects was found a casket containing a miniature portrait of Matilda Hoffman plus a lock of her hair. His burial place: the cemetery at Sleepy Hollow, near where the Headless Horseman rode, or rides.

In the course of his travels, Irving had sketched a lot for the pleasure of it. He had a painter's eye. Noticing this about his books, many distinguished American artists have stretched themselves to illustrate Irving. Among them: Asher Durand, John Quidor, Charles Loring Elliott, Maxfield Parrish and N. C. Wyeth. So Barry Moser's wood-engravings for the present volume continue a most challenging and rewarding tradition.

When all else has been said concerning him, what remains is Irving's particular tone. His voice in both "Rip Van Winkle" and "The Legend of Sleepy Hollow" is like none other in literature. It's extremely supple, witty, sensuous, and fraught with irony of the gentlest, most humane sort. His scenes sparkle with vivid and precise foreground touches; while their middle-distances appear replete with long soft undulations of palpable feeling-thought, which in turn mist backwards to a blue abyss.

He was not a poet, or even a prose-poet, but something more rare than either. He was a sweet-souled wizard in the deliberate

ordering of words, sentences, paragraphs, and indeed whole *xvii*
pages at a go. If painting is "silent poetry," Irving's genius fills the
still woods and vales of our imaginations with some deep, rich
confusion of not-quite-song. Once having harkened to his prose-
music we half-remember it always, like a lulling stream.

So, if you have children about, read these stories aloud to them.
But don't make the error of insisting that your small friends listen
carefully, or that they try to follow what is going on. Let Washington Irving slowly work his own magic spell around them, and
you.

Alexander Eliot, Northampton

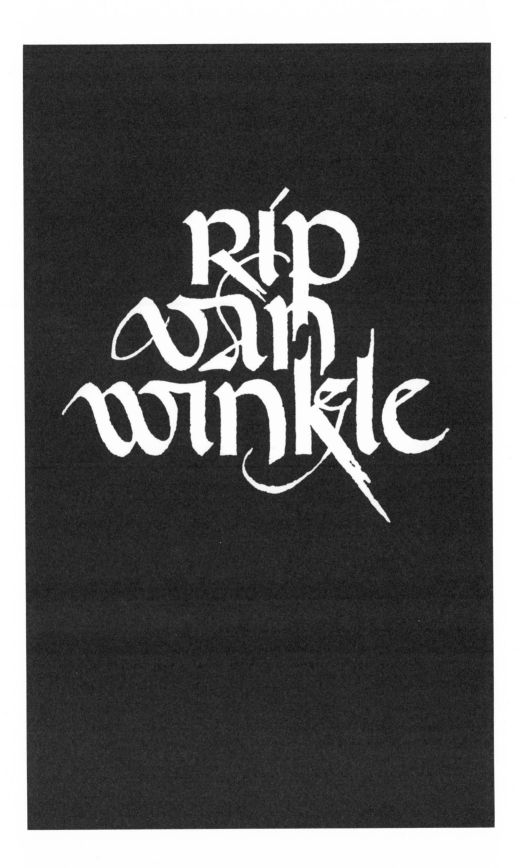

[THE FOLLOWING Tale was found among the papers of the late Diedrich Knickerbocker, an old gentleman of New-York, who was very curious in the Dutch history of the province, and the manners of the descendants from its primitive settlers. His historical researches, however, did not lie so much among books, as among men; for the former are lamentably scanty on his favourite topics; whereas he found the old burghers, and still more, their wives, rich in that legendary lore, so invaluable to true history. Whenever, therefore, he happened upon a genuine Dutch family, snugly shut up in its low-roofed farm house, under a spreading sycamore, he looked upon it as a little clasped volume of black-letter, and studied it with the zeal of a book-worm.

The result of all these researches was a history of the province, during the reign of the Dutch governors, which he published some years since. There have been various opinions as to the literary character of his work, and, to tell the truth, it is not a whit better than it should be. Its chief merit is its scrupulous accuracy, which, indeed, was a little questioned, on its first appearance, but has since been completely established; and it is now admitted into all historical collections, as a book of unquestionable authority.

The old gentleman died shortly after the publication of his work, and now, that he is dead and gone, it cannot do much harm to his memory, to say, that his time might have been much better employed in weightier labours. He, however, was apt to ride his hobby his own way; and though it did now and then kick up the dust a little in the eyes of his neighbours, and grieve the spirit of some friends, for whom he felt the truest deference and affection; yet his errors and follies are remembered "more in sorrow than in anger,"* and it begins to be suspected, that he never intended to injure or offend. But however his memory may be appreciated by critics, it is still held dear among many folk, whose good opinion is well worth having; particularly certain biscuit bakers, who have gone so far as to imprint his likeness on their new year cakes, and have thus given him a chance for immortality, almost equal to being stamped on a Waterloo medal, or a Queen Anne's farthing.]

* Vide the excellent discourse of G. C. Verplanck, Esq. before the New-York Historical Society.

RIP VAN WINKLE.

A Posthumous Writing of Diedrich Knickerbocker.

By Woden, God of Saxons,
From whence comes Wensday, that is Wodensday,
Truth is a thing that ever I will keep
Unto thylke day in which I creep into
My sepulchre—

CARTWRIGHT.

WHOEVER has made a voyage up the Hudson, must re-member the Kaatskill mountains. They are a dismembered branch of the great Appalachian family, and are seen away to the west of the river, swelling up to a noble height, and lording it over the surrounding country. Every change of season, every change of weather, indeed, every hour of the day, produces some change in the magical hues and shapes of these mountains, and they are regarded by all the good wives, far and near, as perfect barom-eters. When the weather is fair and settled, they are clothed in blue and purple, and print their bold outlines on the clear evening sky; but some times, when the rest of the landscape is cloudless, they will gather a hood of gray vapours about their summits, which, in the last rays of the setting sun, will glow and light up like a crown of glory.

At the foot of these fairy mountains, the voyager may have descried the light smoke curling up from a village, whose shingle roofs gleam among the trees, just where the blue tints of the upland melt away into the fresh green of the nearer landscape. It is a little village of great antiquity, having been founded by some of the Dutch colonists, in the early times of the province, just about the beginning of the government of the good Peter Stuyvesant, (may he rest in peace!) and there were some of the houses of the original settlers standing within a few years, with lattice windows, gable fronts surmounted with weathercocks, and built of small yellow bricks brought from Holland.

In that same village, and in one of these very houses, (which, to tell the precise truth, was sadly time worn and weather beaten,) there lived many years since, while the country was yet a province of Great Britain, a simple good natured fellow, of the name of Rip Van Winkle. He was a descendant of the Van Winkles who figured so gallantly in the chivalrous days of Peter Stuyvesant, and accompanied him to the siege of Fort Christina. He inherited, however, but little of the martial character of his ancestors. I have observed that he was a simple good natured man; he was moreover a kind neighbour, and an obedient, henpecked husband. Indeed, to the latter circumstance might be owing that meekness of spirit which gained him such universal popularity; for those men are most apt to be obsequious and conciliating abroad, who are under the discipline of shrews at home. Their tempers, doubtless, are rendered pliant and malleable in the fiery furnace of domestic tribulation, and a curtain lecture is worth all the sermons in the world for teaching the virtues of patience and long suffering. A termagant wife may, therefore, in some respects, be considered a tolerable blessing; and if so, Rip Van Winkle was thrice blessed.

Certain it is, that he was a great favourite among all the good wives of the village, who, as usual with the amiable sex, took his part in all family squabbles, and never failed, whenever they talked those matters over in their evening gossippings, to lay all the blame on Dame Van Winkle. The children of the village, too, would shout with joy whenever he approached. He assisted at their sports, made their playthings, taught them to fly kites and shoot marbles, and told them long stories of ghosts, witches, and Indians. Whenever he went dodging about the village, he was surrounded by a troop of them, hanging on his skirts, clambering

on his back, and playing a thousand tricks on him with impunity; and not a dog would bark at him throughout the neighbourhood.

The great error in Rip's composition was an insuperable aversion to all kinds of profitable labour. It could not be for the want of assiduity or perseverance; for he would sit on a wet rock, with a rod as long and heavy as a Tartar's lance, and fish all day without a murmur, even though he should not be encouraged by a single nibble. He would carry a fowling piece on his shoulder, for hours together, trudging through woods and swamps, and up hill and down dale, to shoot a few squirrels or wild pigeons. He would never even refuse to assist a neighbour in the roughest toil, and was a foremost man at all country frolicks for husking Indian corn, or building stone fences. The women of the village, too, used to employ him to run their errands, and to do such little odd jobs as their less obliging husbands would not do for them;–in a word, Rip was ready to attend to any body's business but his own; but as to doing family duty, and keeping his farm in order, it was impossible.

In fact, he declared it was no use to work on his farm; it was the most pestilent little piece of ground in the whole country; every thing about it went wrong, and would go wrong, in spite of him. His fences were continually falling to pieces; his cow would either go astray, or get among the cabbages; weeds were sure to grow quicker in his fields than any where else; the rain always made a point of setting in just as he had some out-door work to do; so that though his patrimonial estate had dwindled away under his management, acre by acre, until there was little more left than a mere patch of Indian corn and potatoes, yet it was the worst conditioned farm in the neighbourhood.

His children, too, were as ragged and wild as if they belonged to nobody. His son Rip, an urchin begotten in his own likeness, promised to inherit the habits, with the old clothes of his father. He was generally seen trooping like a colt at his mother's heels, equipped in a pair of his father's cast-off galligaskins, which he had much ado to hold up with one hand, as a fine lady does her train in bad weather.

Rip Van Winkle, however, was one of those happy mortals, of

6 foolish, well-oiled dispositions, who take the world easy, eat white bread or brown, whichever can be got with least thought or trouble, and would rather starve on a penny than work for a pound. If left to himself, he would have whistled life away, in perfect contentment; but his wife kept continually dinning in his ears about his idleness, his carelessness, and the ruin he was bringing on his family. Morning, noon, and night, her tongue was incessantly going, and every thing he said or did was sure to produce a torrent of household eloquence. Rip had but one way of replying to all lectures of the kind, and that, by frequent use, had grown into a habit. He shrugged his shoulders, shook his head, cast up his eyes, but said nothing. This, however, always provoked a fresh volley from his wife, so that he was fain to draw off his forces, and take to the outside of the house—the only side which, in truth, belongs to a henpecked husband.

Rip's sole domestic adherent was his dog Wolf, who was as much henpecked as his master; for Dame Van Winkle regarded them as companions in idleness, and even looked upon Wolf with an evil eye, as the cause of his master's so often going astray. True it is, in all points of spirit befitting an honourable dog, he was as courageous an animal as ever scoured the woods—but what courage can withstand the ever-during and all-besetting terrors of a woman's tongue? The moment Wolf entered the house, his crest fell, his tail drooped to the ground, or curled between his legs, he sneaked about with a gallows air, casting many a sidelong glance at Dame Van Winkle, and at the least flourish of a broomstick or ladle, would fly to the door with yelping precipitation.

Times grew worse and worse with Rip Van Winkle as years of matrimony rolled on; a tart temper never mellows with age, and a sharp tongue is the only edge tool that grows keener by constant use. For a long while he used to console himself, when driven from home, by frequenting a kind of perpetual club of the sages, philosophers, and other idle personages of the village, which held its sessions on a bench before a small inn, designated by a rubicund portrait of his majesty George the Third. Here they used to sit in the shade, of a long lazy summer's day, talk listlessly over village gossip, or tell endless sleepy stories about nothing. But it

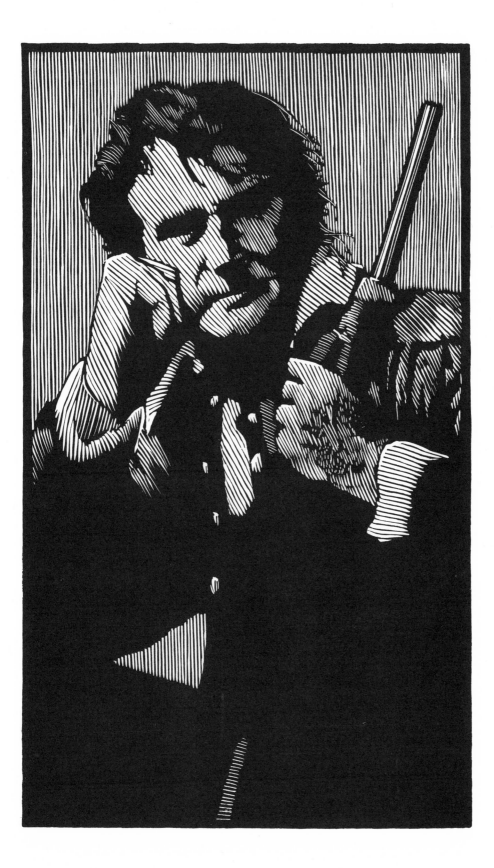

would have been worth any statesman's money to have heard the
profound discussions that sometimes took place, when by chance
an old newspaper fell into their hands, from some passing traveller. How solemnly they would listen to the contents, as drawled
out by Derrick Van Bummel, the schoolmaster, a dapper learned
little man, who was not to be daunted by the most gigantic word
in the dictionary; and how sagely they would deliberate upon
public events some months after they had taken place.

The opinions of this junto were completely controlled by
Nicholas Vedder, a patriarch of the village, and landlord of the
inn, at the door of which he took his seat from morning till night,
just moving sufficiently to avoid the sun, and keep in the shade of
a large tree; so that the neighbours could tell the hour by his
movements as accurately as by a sun dial. It is true, he was rarely
heard to speak, but smoked his pipe incessantly. His adherents,
however, (for every great man has his adherents,) perfectly understood him, and knew how to gather his opinions. When any thing
that was read or related displeased him, he was observed to smoke
his pipe vehemently, and send forth short, frequent, and angry
puffs; but when pleased, he would inhale the smoke slowly and
tranquilly, and emit it in light and placid clouds, and sometimes
taking the pipe from his mouth, and letting the fragrant vapour
curl about his nose, would gravely nod his head in token of perfect
approbation.

From even this strong hold the unlucky Rip was at length
routed by his termagant wife, who would suddenly break in upon
the tranquillity of the assemblage, call the members all to nought;
nor was that august personage, Nicholas Vedder himself, sacred
from the daring tongue of this terrible virago, who charged him
outright with encouraging her husband in habits of idleness.

Poor Rip was at last reduced almost to despair; and his only
alternative to escape from the labour of the farm and the clamour
of his wife, was to take gun in hand, and stroll away into the
woods. Here he would sometimes seat himself at the foot of a tree,
and share the contents of his wallet with Wolf, with whom he
sympathised as a fellow sufferer in persecution. "Poor Wolf," he
would say, "thy mistress leads thee a dog's life of it; but never

8 mind, my lad, while I live thou shalt never want a friend to stand by thee!" Wolf would wag his tail, look wistfully in his master's face, and if dogs can feel pity, I verily believe he reciprocated the sentiment with all his heart.

In a long ramble of the kind on a fine autumnal day, Rip had unconsciously scrambled to one of the highest parts of the Kaats-kill mountains. He was after his favourite sport of squirrel shoot-ing, and the still solitudes had echoed and re-echoed with the reports of his gun. Panting and fatigued, he threw himself, late in the afternoon, on a green knoll, covered with mountain herbage, that crowned the brow of a precipice. From an opening between the trees, he could overlook all the lower country for many a mile of rich woodland. He saw at a distance the lordly Hudson, far, far below him, moving on its silent but majestic course, the reflection of a purple cloud, or the sail of a lagging bark, here and there sleeping on its glassy bosom, and at last losing itself in the blue highlands.

On the other side he looked down into a deep mountain glen, wild, lonely, and shagged, the bottom filled with fragments from the impending cliffs, and scarcely lighted by the reflected rays of the setting sun. For some time Rip lay musing on this scene; evening was gradually advancing, the mountains began to throw their long blue shadows over the valleys, he saw that it would be dark long before he could reach the village, and he heaved a heavy sigh when he thought of encountering the terrors of Dame Van Winkle.

As he was about to descend, he heard a voice from a distance, hallooing, "Rip Van Winkle! Rip Van Winkle!" He looked around, but could see nothing but a crow winging its solitary flight across the mountain. He thought his fancy must have de-ceived him, and turned again to descend, when he heard the same cry ring through the still evening air; "Rip Van Winkle! Rip Van Winkle!"–at the same time Wolf bristled up his back, and giving a low growl, skulked to his master's side, looking fearfully down into the glen. Rip now felt a vague apprehension stealing over him; he looked anxiously in the same direction, and perceived a strange figure slowly toiling up the rocks, and bending under the

weight of something he carried on his back. He was surprised to   9
see any human being in this lonely and unfrequented place, but
supposing it to be some one of the neighbourhood in need of his
assistance, he hastened down to yield it.

On nearer approach, he was still more surprised at the singular-
ity of the stranger's appearance. He was a short square built old
fellow, with thick bushy hair, and a grizzled beard. His dress was
of the antique Dutch fashion–a cloth jerkin strapped round the
waist–several pair of breeches, the outer one of ample volume,
decorated with rows of buttons down the sides, and bunches at
the knees. He bore on his shoulder a stout keg, that seemed full of
liquor, and made signs for Rip to approach and assist him with the
load. Though rather shy and distrustful of this new acquaintance,
Rip complied with his usual alacrity, and mutually relieving each
other, they clambered up a narrow gully, apparently the dry bed
of a mountain torrent. As they ascended, Rip every now and then
heard long rolling peals, like distant thunder, that seemed to issue
out of a deep ravine, or rather cleft between lofty rocks, toward
which their rugged path conducted. He paused for an instant, but
supposing it to be the muttering of one of those transient thunder
showers which often take place in mountain heights, he pro-
ceeded. Passing through the ravine, they came to a hollow, like a
small amphitheatre, surrounded by perpendicular precipices, over
the brinks of which impending trees shot their branches, so that
you only caught glimpses of the azure sky, and the bright evening
cloud. During the whole time, Rip and his companion had la-
boured on in silence; for though the former marvelled greatly
what could be the object of carrying a keg of liquor up this wild
mountain, yet there was something strange and incomprehensible
about the unknown, that inspired awe, and checked familiarity.

On entering the amphitheatre, new objects of wonder presented themselves. On a level spot in the centre was a company of
odd-looking personages playing at nine-pins. They were dressed
in a quaint, outlandish fashion: some wore short doublets, others
jerkins, with long knives in their belts, and most had enormous
breeches, of similar style with that of the guide's. Their visages,
too, were peculiar: one had a large head, broad face, and small

piggish eyes; the face of another seemed to consist entirely of nose, and was surmounted by a white sugar-loaf hat, set off with a little red cockstail. They all had beards, of various shapes and colours. There was one who seemed to be the commander. He was a stout old gentleman, with a weather-beaten countenance: he wore a laced doublet, broad belt and hanger, high crowned hat and feather, red stockings, and high heeled shoes, with roses in them. The whole group reminded Rip of the figures in an old Flemish painting, in the parlour of Dominie Van Schaick, the village parson, and which had been brought over from Holland at the time of the settlement.

What seemed particularly odd to Rip, was, that though these folks were evidently amusing themselves, yet they maintained the gravest faces, the most mysterious silence, and were, withal, the most melancholy party of pleasure he had ever witnessed. Nothing interrupted the stillness of the scene, but the noise of the balls, which, whenever they were rolled, echoed along the mountains like rumbling peals of thunder.

As Rip and his companion approached them, they suddenly desisted from their play, and stared at him with such fixed statue-like gaze, and such strange, uncouth, lack lustre countenances, that his heart turned within him, and his knees smote together. His companion now emptied the contents of the keg into large flagons, and made signs to him to wait upon the company. He obeyed with fear and trembling; they quaffed the liquor in profound silence, and then returned to their game.

By degrees, Rip's awe and apprehension subsided. He even ventured, when no eye was fixed upon him, to taste the beverage, which he found had much of the flavour of excellent Hollands. He was naturally a thirsty soul, and was soon tempted to repeat the draught. One taste provoked another, and he reiterated his visits to the flagon so often, that at length his senses were overpowered, his eyes swam in his head, his head gradually declined, and he fell into a deep sleep.

On awaking, he found himself on the green knoll from whence he had first seen the old man of the glen. He rubbed his eyes—it was a bright sunny morning. The birds were hopping and twitter-

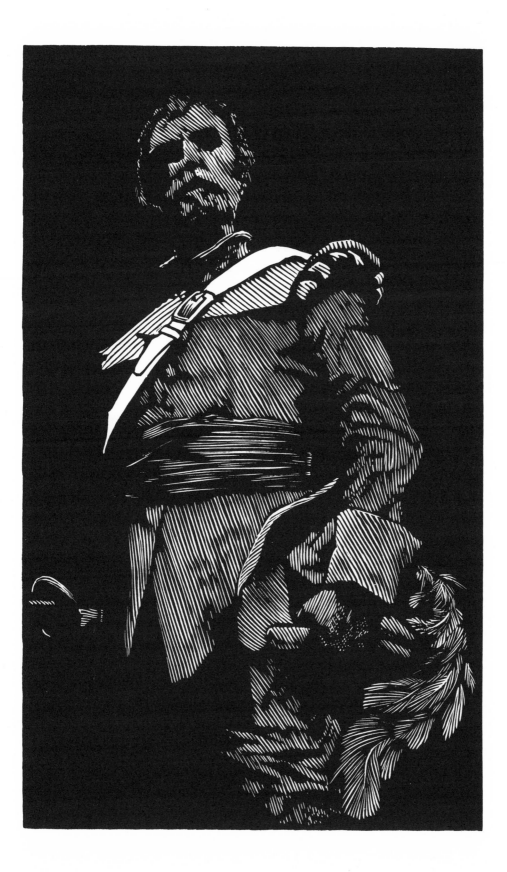

ing among the bushes, and the eagle was wheeling aloft, and breasting the pure mountain breeze. "Surely," thought Rip, "I have not slept here all night." He recalled the occurrences before he fell asleep. The strange man with the keg of liquor–the mountain ravine–the wild retreat among the rocks–the wo-begone party at nine-pins–the flagon–"Oh! that flagon! that wicked flagon!" thought Rip–"what excuse shall I make to Dame Van Winkle?"

He looked round for his gun, but in place of the clean well-oiled fowling-piece, he found an old firelock lying by him, the barrel encrusted with rust, the lock falling off, and the stock worm-eaten. He now suspected that the grave roysters of the mountain had put a trick upon him, and having dosed him with liquor, had robbed him of his gun. Wolf, too, had disappeared, but he might have strayed away after a squirrel or partridge. He whistled after him, shouted his name, but all in vain; the echoes repeated his whistle and shout, but no dog was to be seen.

He determined to revisit the scene of the last evening's gambol, and if he met with any of the party, to demand his dog and gun. As he arose to walk, he found himself stiff in the joints, and wanting in his usual activity. "These mountain beds do not agree with me," thought Rip, "and if this frolick should lay me up with a fit of the rheumatism, I shall have a blessed time with Dame Van Winkle." With some difficulty he got down into the glen; he found the gully up which he and his companion had ascended the preceding evening; but to his astonishment a mountain stream was now foaming down it, leaping from rock to rock, and filling the glen with babbling murmurs. He, however, made shift to scramble up its sides, working his toilsome way through thickets of birch, sassafras, and witch hazle, and sometimes tripped up or entangled by the wild grape vines that twisted their coils and tendrils from tree to tree, and spread a kind of network in his path.

At length he reached to where the ravine had opened through the cliffs, to the amphitheatre; but no traces of such opening remained. The rocks presented a high impenetrable wall, over which the torrent came tumbling in a sheet of feathery foam, and fell into a broad deep basin, black from the shadows of the surrounding forest. Here, then, poor Rip was brought to a stand. He again called and whistled after his dog; he was only answered by the cawing of a flock of idle crows, sporting high in air about a dry tree that overhung a sunny precipice; and who, secure in their elevation, seemed to look down and scoff at the poor man's perplexities. What was to be done? the morning was passing away, and Rip felt famished for his breakfast. He grieved to give up his dog and gun; he dreaded to meet his wife; but it would not do to starve among the mountains. He shook his head, shouldered the rusty firelock, and, with a heart full of trouble and anxiety, turned his steps homeward.

As he approached the village, he met a number of people, but none whom he knew, which somewhat surprised him, for he had thought himself acquainted with every one in the country round. Their dress, too, was of a different fashion from that to which he was accustomed. They all stared at him with equal marks of surprise, and whenever they cast eyes upon him, invariably stroked their chins. The constant recurrence of this gesture induced Rip, involuntarily, to do the same, when, to his astonishment, he found his beard had grown a foot long!

He had now entered the skirts of the village. A troop of strange children ran at his heels, hooting after him, and pointing at his gray beard. The dogs, too, not one of which he recognized for his old acquaintances, barked at him as he passed. The very village seemed altered: it was larger and more populous. There were rows of houses which he had never seen before, and those which had been his familiar haunts had disappeared. Strange names were over the doors–strange faces at the windows–every thing was strange. His mind now began to misgive him, that both he and the world around him were bewitched. Surely this was his native village, which he had left but the day before. There stood the Kaatskill mountains–there ran the silver Hudson at a distance–there was every hill and dale precisely as it had always been–Rip was sorely perplexed–"That flagon last night," thought he, "has addled my poor head sadly!"

It was with some difficulty he found the way to his own house, which he approached with silent awe, expecting every moment to

hear the shrill voice of Dame Van Winkle. He found the house gone to decay–the roof fallen in, the windows shattered, and the doors off the hinges. A half starved dog, that looked like Wolf, was skulking about it. Rip called him by name, but the cur snarled, showed his teeth, and passed on. This was an unkind cut indeed–"My very dog," sighed poor Rip, "has forgotten me!"

He entered the house, which, to tell the truth, Dame Van Winkle had always kept in neat order. It was empty, forlorn, and apparently abandoned. This desolateness overcame all his connubial fears–he called loudly for his wife and children–the lonely chambers rung for a moment with his voice, and then all again was silence.

He now hurried forth, and hastened to his old resort, the little village inn–but it too was gone. A large ricketty wooden building stood in its place, with great gaping windows, some of them broken, and mended with old hats and petticoats, and over the door was painted, "The Union Hotel, by Jonathan Doolittle." Instead of the great tree that used to shelter the quiet little Dutch inn of yore, there now was reared a tall naked pole, with something on top that looked like a red night cap, and from it was fluttering a flag, on which was a singular assemblage of stars and stripes–all this was strange and incomprehensible. He recognised on the sign, however, the ruby face of King George, under which he had smoked so many a peaceful pipe, but even this was singularly metamorphosed. The red coat was changed for one of blue and buff, a sword was stuck in the hand instead of a sceptre, the head was decorated with a cocked hat, and underneath was painted in large characters, GENERAL WASHINGTON.

There was, as usual, a crowd of folk about the door, but none whom Rip recollected. The very character of the people seemed changed. There was a busy, bustling, disputatious tone about it, instead of the accustomed phlegm and drowsy tranquillity. He looked in vain for the sage Nicholas Vedder, with his broad face, double chin, and fair long pipe, uttering clouds of tobacco smoke instead of idle speeches; or Van Bummel, the schoolmaster, doling forth the contents of an ancient newspaper. In place of these, a lean bilious looking fellow, with his pockets full of handbills, was haranguing vehemently about rights of citizens–election–members of congress–liberty–Bunker's hill–heroes of seventy-six–and other words, that were a perfect Babylonish jargon to the bewildered Van Winkle.

The appearance of Rip, with his long grizzled beard, his rusty fowling piece, his uncouth dress, and the army of women and children that had gathered at his heels, soon attracted the attention of the tavern politicians. They crowded around him, eyeing him from head to foot, with great curiosity. The orator bustled up to him, and drawing him partly aside, inquired "which side he voted?" Rip stared in vacant stupidity. Another short but busy little fellow pulled him by the arm, and raising on tiptoe, inquired in his ear, "whether he was Federal or Democrat." Rip was equally at a loss to comprehend the question; when a knowing, self-important old gentleman, in a sharp cocked hat, made his way through the crowd, putting them to the right and left with his elbows as he passed, and planting himself before Van Winkle, with one arm akimbo, the other resting on his cane, his keen eyes and sharp hat penetrating, as it were, into his very soul, demanded, in an austere tone, "what brought him to the election with a gun on his shoulder, and a mob at his heels, and whether he meant to breed a riot in the village?" "Alas! gentlemen," cried Rip, somewhat dismayed, "I am a poor quiet man, a native of the place, and a loyal subject of the King, God bless him!"

Here a general shout burst from the bystanders–"A tory! a tory! a spy! a refugee! hustle him! away with him!" It was with great difficulty that the self-important man in the cocked hat restored order; and having assumed a tenfold austerity of brow, demanded again of the unknown culprit, what he came there for, and whom he was seeking. The poor man humbly assured him that he meant no harm; but merely came there in search of some of his neighbours, who used to keep about the tavern.

"Well–who are they?–name them."

Rip bethought himself a moment, and inquired, "where's Nicholas Vedder?"

There was a silence for a little while, when an old man replied, in a thin piping voice, "Nicholas Vedder? why he is dead and gone these eighteen years! There was a wooden tombstone in the church yard that used to tell all about him, but that's rotted and gone too."

"Where's Brom Dutcher?"

"Oh, he went off to the army in the beginning of the war; some say he was killed at the battle of Stoney-Point–others say he was drowned in a squall, at the foot of Antony's Nose. I don't know– he never came back again."

"Where's Van Bummel, the schoolmaster?"

"He went off to the wars too, was a great militia general, and is now in Congress."

Rip's heart died away, at hearing of these sad changes in his home and friends, and finding himself thus alone in the world. Every answer puzzled him, too, by treating of such enormous lapses of time, and of matters which he could not understand: war–Congress–Stoney Point!–he had no courage to ask after any more friends, but cried out in despair, "does nobody here know Rip Van Winkle?"

"Oh, Rip Van Winkle!" exclaimed two or three, "Oh, to be sure! that's Rip Van Winkle yonder, leaning against the tree."

Rip looked, and beheld a precise counterpart of himself, as he went up the mountain: apparently as lazy, and certainly as ragged. The poor fellow was now completely confounded. He doubted his own identity, and whether he was himself or another man. In the midst of his bewilderment, the man in the cocked hat demanded who he was, and what was his name?

"God knows," exclaimed he, at his wit's end; "I'm not myself– I'm somebody else–that's me yonder–no–that's somebody else, got into my shoes–I was myself last night, but I fell asleep on the mountain, and they've changed my gun, and every thing's changed, and I'm changed, and I can't tell what's my name, or who I am!"

The bystanders began now to look at each other, nod, wink significantly, and tap their fingers against their foreheads. There was a whisper, also, about securing the gun, and keeping the old fellow from doing mischief; at the very suggestion of which, the self-important man in the cocked hat retired with some precipitation. At this critical moment a fresh likely woman pressed through the throng to get a peep at the graybearded man. She had a chubby child in her arms, which, frightened at his looks, began to cry. "Hush, Rip," cried she, "hush, you little fool, the old man wont hurt you." The name of the child, the air of the mother, the tone of her voice, all awakened a train of recollections in his mind.

"What is your name, my good woman?" asked he.

"Judith Gardenier."

"And your father's name?"

"Ah, poor man, his name was Rip Van Winkle; it's twenty years since he went away from home with his gun, and never has been heard of since–his dog came home without him; but whether he shot himself, or was carried away by the Indians, nobody can tell. I was then but a little girl."

Rip had but one question more to ask; but he put it with a faltering voice:

"Where's your mother?"

Oh, she too had died but a short time since; she broke a blood vessel in a fit of passion at a New-England peddler.

There was a drop of comfort, at least, in this intelligence. The honest man could contain himself no longer.–He caught his daughter and her child in his arms.–"I am your father!" cried he–"Young Rip Van Winkle once–old Rip Van Winkle now!–Does nobody know poor Rip Van Winkle!"

All stood amazed, until an old woman, tottering out from among the crowd, put her hand to her brow, and peering under it in his face for a moment, exclaimed, "Sure enough! it is Rip Van Winkle–it is himself. Welcome home again, old neighbour–Why, where have you been these twenty long years?"

Rip's story was soon told, for the whole twenty years had been to him but as one night. The neighbours stared when they heard it; some were seen to wink at each other, and put their tongues in their cheeks; and the self-important man in the cocked hat, who, when the alarm was over, had returned to the field, screwed down the corners of his mouth, and shook his head–upon which there was a general shaking of the head throughout the assemblage.

It was determined, however, to take the opinion of old Peter

Vanderdonk, who was seen slowly advancing up the road. He was a descendant of the historian of that name, who wrote one of the earliest accounts of the province. Peter was the most ancient inhabitant of the village, and well versed in all the wonderful events and traditions of the neighbourhood. He recollected Rip at once, and corroborated his story in the most satisfactory manner. He assured the company that it was a fact, handed down from his ancestor the historian, that the Kaatskill mountains had always been haunted by strange beings. That it was affirmed that the great Hendrick Hudson, the first discoverer of the river and country, kept a kind of vigil there every twenty years, with his crew of the Half-moon, being permitted in this way to revisit the scenes of his enterprize, and keep a guardian eye upon the river, and the great city called by his name. That his father had once seen them in their old Dutch dresses playing at nine pins in a hollow of the mountain; and that he himself had heard, one summer afternoon, the sound of their balls, like long peals of thunder.

To make a long story short, the company broke up, and returned to the more important concerns of the election. Rip's daughter took him home to live with her; she had a snug, well-furnished house, and a stout cheery farmer for a husband, whom Rip recollected for one of the urchins that used to climb upon his back. As to Rip's son and heir, who was the ditto of himself, seen leaning against the tree, he was employed to work on the farm; but evinced an hereditary disposition to attend to any thing else but his business.

Rip now resumed his old walks and habits; he soon found many of his former cronies, though all rather the worse for the wear and tear of time; and preferred making friends among the rising generation, with whom he soon grew into great favour.

Having nothing to do at home, and being arrived at that happy age when a man can do nothing with impunity, he took his place once more on the bench, at the inn door, and was reverenced as one of the patriarchs of the village, and a chronicle of the old times "before the war." It was some time before he could get into the regular track of gossip, or could be made to comprehend the strange events that had taken place during his torpor; how that there had been a revolutionary war—that the country had thrown off the yoke of old England—and that, instead of being a subject of his Majesty George the Third, he was now a free citizen of the United States. Rip, in fact, was no politician; the changes of states and empires made but little impression on him. But there was one species of despotism under which he had long groaned, and that was—petticoat government: happily, that was at an end; he had got his neck out of the yoke of matrimony, and could go in and out whenever he pleased, without dreading the tyranny of Dame Van Winkle. Whenever her name was mentioned, however, he shook his head, shrugged his shoulders, and cast up his eyes; which might pass either for an expression of resignation to his fate, or joy at his deliverance.

He used to tell his story to every stranger that arrived at Mr. Doolittle's hotel. He was observed, at first, to vary on some points every time he told it, which was, doubtless, owing to his having so recently awaked. It at last settled down precisely to the tale I have related, and not a man, woman, or child in the neighbourhood, but knew it by heart. Some always pretended to doubt the reality of it, and insisted that Rip had been out of his head, and that this was one point on which he always remained flighty. The old Dutch inhabitants, however, almost universally gave it full credit. Even to this day they never hear a thunder storm of a summer afternoon, about the Kaatskill, but they say Hendrick Hudson and his crew are at their game of nine pins; and it is a common wish of all henpecked husbands in the neighbourhood, when life hangs heavy on their hands, that they might have a quieting draught out of Rip Van Winkle's flagon.

NOTE.

The foregoing tale, one would suspect, had been suggested to Mr. Knicker-bocker by a little German superstition about Charles V. and the Kypphauser mountain; the subjoined note, however, which he had appended to the tale, shows that it is an absolute fact, narrated with his usual fidelity.

"The story of Rip Van Winkle may seem incredible to many, but neverthe-less I give it my full belief, for I know the vicinity of our old Dutch settle-ments to have been very subject to marvellous events and appearances. In-deed, I have heard many stranger stories than this, in the villages along the Hudson; all of which were too well authenticated to admit of a doubt. I have even talked with Rip Van Winkle myself, who, when last I saw him, was a very venerable old man, and so perfectly rational and consistent on every other point, that I think no conscientious person could refuse to take this into the bargain; nay, I have seen a certificate on the subject taken before a country justice and signed with a cross, in the justice's own hand writing. The story, therefore, is beyond the possibility of doubt.

"D.K."

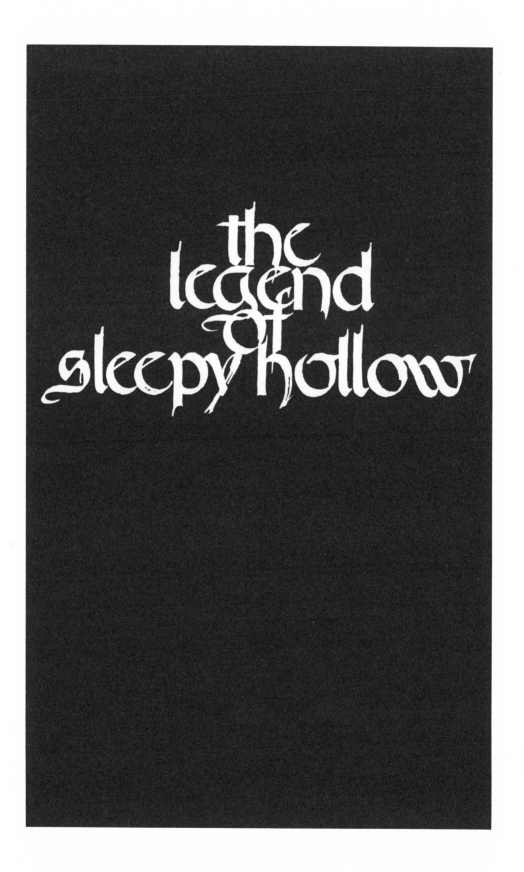

THE LEGEND OF SLEEPY HOLLOW.

(Found Among the Papers of the Late Diedrich Knickerbocker.)

A pleasing land of drowsy head it was,
Of dreams that wave before the half-shut eye;
And of gay castles in the clouds that pass,
Forever flushing round a summer sky.

CASTLE OF INDOLENCE.

IN THE bosom of one of the spacious coves which indent the eastern shore of the Hudson, at the broad expansion of the river denominated by the ancient Dutch navigators the Tappaan Zee, and where they always prudently shortened sail, and implored the protection of St. Nicholas when they crossed, there lies a small market town or rural port, which by some is called Greensburgh, but which is more universally and properly known by the name of Tarry Town. This name was given it, we are told, in former days, by the good housewives of the adjacent country, from the inveterate propensity of their husbands to linger about the village tavern on market days. Be that as it may, I do not vouch for the fact, but merely advert to it, for the sake of being precise and authentic. Not far from this village, perhaps about three miles, there is a little valley, or rather lap of land among high hills, which is one of the quietest places in the whole world. A small brook glides through it, with just murmur enough to lull you to repose, and the occasional whistle of a quail, or tapping of a woodpecker, is almost the only sound that ever breaks in upon the uniform tranquillity.

I recollect that when a stripling, my first exploit in squirrel shooting was in a grove of tall wallnut trees that shades one side of the valley. I had wandered into it at noon time, when all nature is peculiarly quiet, and was startled by the roar of my own gun, as it broke the sabbath stillness around, and was prolonged and reverberated by the angry echoes. If ever I should wish for a retreat, whither I might steal from the world and its distractions, and dream quietly away the remnant of a troubled life, I know of none more promising than this little valley.

From the listless repose of the place, and the peculiar character of its inhabitants, who are descendants from the original Dutch settlers, this sequestered glen has long been known by the name of SLEEPY HOLLOW, and its rustic lads are called the Sleepy Hollow Boys throughout all the neighbouring country. A drowsy, dreamy influence seems to hang over the land, and pervade the very atmosphere. Some say that the place was bewitched by a high German doctor during the early days of the settlement; others, that an old Indian chief, the prophet or wizard of his tribe, held his powwows there before the country was discovered by Master Hendrick Hudson. Certain it is, the place still continues under the sway of some witching power, that holds a spell over the minds of the good people, causing them to walk in a continual reverie. They are given to all kinds of marvellous beliefs; have trances and visions, and see strange sights, and hear music and voices in the air. The whole neighbourhood abounds with local tales, haunted spots, and twilight superstitions; stars shoot and meteors glare oftener across the valley than in any other part of the country, and the night-mare, with her whole nine fold, seems to make it the favourite scene of her gambols.

The dominant spirit, however, that haunts this enchanted region, and seems to be commander of all the powers of the air, is the apparition of a figure on horseback without a head. It is said by some to be the ghost of a Hessian trooper, whose head had been carried away by a cannon-ball, in some nameless battle during the

revolutionary war, and who is ever and anon seen by various of the country people, hurrying along in the gloom of night, as if on the wings of the wind. His haunts are not confined to the valley, but extend at times to the adjacent roads, and especially to the vicinity of a church that is at no great distance. Indeed, certain of the most authentic historians of those parts, who have been careful in collecting and collating the floating facts concerning this spectre, allege, that the body of the trooper having been buried in the church-yard, the ghost rides forth to the scene of battle in nightly quest of his head, and the rushing speed with which he sometimes passes along the hollow, like a midnight blast, is owing to his being belated, and in a hurry to get back to the church-yard before day-break.

Such is the general purport of this legendary superstition, which has furnished materials for many a wild story in that region of shadows; and the spectre is known at all the country firesides, by the name of The Headless Horseman of Sleepy Hollow.

It is remarkable, that the visionary turn I have mentioned is not confined to the native inhabitants of the valley, but is imperceptibly acquired by every one who resides there for a time. However wide awake they may have been before they entered that sleepy region, they are sure, in a little time, to imbibe the witching influence of the air, and begin to grow imaginative–to dream dreams, and see apparitions.

I mention this peaceful spot with all possible laud; for it is in such little retired Dutch valleys, found here and there embosomed in the great state of New-York, that populations, manners, and customs, remained fixed, while the great torrent of emigration and improvement, which is making such incessant changes in other parts of this restless country, sweeps by them unobserved. They are like those little nooks of still water, which border a rapid stream, where we may see the straw and bubble riding quietly at anchor, or slowly revolving in their mimic harbour, undisturbed by the rushing of the passing current. Though many years have elapsed since I trod the drowsy shades of Sleepy Hollow, yet I question whether I should not still find the same trees and the same families vegetating in its sheltered bosom.

26

In this by-place of nature there abode, in a remote period of American history, that is to say, some thirty years since, a worthy wight of the name of Ichabod Crane, who sojourned, or, as he expressed it, "tarried," in Sleepy Hollow, for the purpose of instructing the children of the vicinity. He was a native of Connecticut, a state which supplies the Union with pioneers for the mind as well as the forest, and sends forth yearly its legions of frontier woodmen and country schoolmasters. The cognomen of Crane was not inapplicable to his person. He was tall, but exceedingly lank, with narrow shoulders, long arms and legs, hands that dangled a mile out of his sleeves, feet that might have served for shovels, and his whole frame most loostly hung together. His head was small, and flat at top, with huge ears, large green glassy eyes, and a long snipe nose, so that it might have been mistaken for a weathercock perched upon his spindle neck, to tell which way the wind blew. To see him striding along the profile of a hill on a windy day, with his clothes bagging and fluttering about him, one might have mistaken him for the genius of famine descending upon the earth, or some scarecrow eloped from a cornfield.

His school-house was a low building of one large room, rudely constructed of logs; the windows partly glazed, and partly patched with leaves of old copy books. It was most ingeniously secured at vacant hours, by a withe twisted in the handle of the door, and stakes set against the window shutters; so that though a thief might get in with perfect ease, he would find some embarrassment in getting out; an idea most probably borrowed by the architect, Yost Van Houten, from the mystery of an eelpot. The school-house stood in rather a lonely but a pleasant situation, just at the foot of a woody hill, with a brook running close by, and a formidable birch tree growing at one end of it. From hence the low murmur of his pupil's voices, conning over their lessons, might be heard of a drowsy summer's day, like the hum of a bee-hive; interrupted now and then by the authoritative voice of the master, giving menace or command, or, peradventure, the appalling sound of the birch, as he urged some tardy loiterer along the flowery path of knowledge. Truth to say, he was a conscien-

tious man, that ever bore in mind the golden maxim, "spare the rod and spoil the child."–Ichabod Crane's scholars certainly were not spoiled.

I would not have it imagined, however, that he was one of those cruel potentates of the school, who joy in the smart of their subjects; on the contrary, he administered justice with discrimination rather than severity; taking the burthen off the backs of the weak, and laying it on those of the strong. Your mere puny stripling, that winced at the least flourish of the rod, was passed by with indulgence; but the claims of justice were satisfied, by giving a double portion to some little, tough, wrong-headed, broad-skirted Dutch urchin, who sulked and swelled and grew dogged and sullen beneath the birch. All this he called "doing his duty by their parents;" and he never inflicted a chastisement without following it by the assurance, so consolatory to the smarting urchin, that he would remember it and thank him for it the longest day he had to live.

When school hours were over, he was even the companion and playmate of his larger boys; and would convoy some of the smaller ones home of a holyday, who happened to have pretty sisters, or good housewives for mothers, noted for the comforts of the cupboard. Indeed, it behooved him to keep on good terms with his pupils. The revenue arising from his school was small, and would have been scarcely sufficient to furnish him with daily bread, for he was a huge feeder, and though lank, had the dilating powers of an Anaconda; but to help out his maintenance, he was, according to country custom in those parts, boarded and lodged at the houses of the farmers, whose children he instructed. With these he lived alternately a week at a time, thus going the rounds of the neighbourhood, with all his worldly effects tied up in a cotton handkerchief.

That all this might not be too onerous on the purses of his rustic patrons, who are apt to consider the costs of schooling a grievous burthen, and schoolmasters mere drones, he had various ways of rendering himself both useful and agreeable. He assisted the farmers occasionally in the light labours of their farms, helped to make hay, mended the fences, took the horses to water, drove the cows

28 from pasture, and cut wood for the winter fire. He laid aside, too, all the dominant dignity and absolute sway, with which he lorded it in his little empire, the school, and became wonderfully gentle and ingratiating. He found favour in the eyes of the mothers, by petting the children, particularly the youngest, and like the lion bold, which whilome so magnanimously the lamb did hold, he would sit with a child on one knee, and rock a cradle with his foot, for whole hours together.

In addition to his other vocations, he was the singing master of the neighbourhood, and picked up many bright shillings by instructing the young folks in psalmody. It was a matter of no little vanity to him on Sundays, to take his station in front of the church gallery, with a band of chosen singers; where, in his own mind, he completely carried away the palm from the parson. Certain it is, his voice resounded far above all the rest of the congregation, and there are peculiar quavers still to be heard in that church, and which may even be heard half-a-mile off, quite to the opposite side of the mill-pond, of a still Sunday morning, which are said to be legitimately descended from the nose of Ichabod Crane. Thus, by diverse little make shifts, in that ingenious way which is commonly denominated "by hook and by crook," the worthy pedagogue got on tolerably enough, and was thought, by all those who understood nothing of the labour of headwork, to have a wonderful easy life of it.

The schoolmaster is generally a man of some importance in the female circle of a rural neighbourhood, being considered a kind of idle gentleman-like personage, of vastly superior taste and accomplishments to the rough country swains, and, indeed, inferior in learning only to the parson. His appearance, therefore, is apt to occasion some little stir at the tea-table of a farm-house, and the addition of a supernumerary dish of cakes or sweetmeets, or, peradventure, the parade of a silver tea-pot. Our man of letters, therefore, was peculiarly happy in the smiles of all the country damsels. How he would figure among them in the church-yard, between services on Sundays; gathering grapes for them from the wild vines that overrun the surrounding trees; reciting for them all the epitaphs on the tomb-stones, or sauntering, with a whole

bevy of them, along the banks of the adjacent mill-pond; while the 29
more bashful country bumpkins hung sheepishly back, envying
his superior elegance and address.

From his half itinerant life, also, he was a kind of travelling
gazette, carrying the whole budget of local gossip from house to
house; so that his appearance was always greeted with satisfac-
tion. He was, moreover, esteemed by the women as a man of great
erudition, for he had read several books quite through, and was
a perfect master of Cotton Mather's History of New-England
Witchcraft, in which, by the way, he most firmly and potently
believed.

He was, in fact, an odd mixture of small shrewdness and simple
credulity. His appetite for the marvellous, and his powers of di-
gesting it, were equally extraordinary; and both had been increased by his residence in this spell-bound region. No tale was
too gross or monstrous for his capacious swallow. It was often his
delight, after his school was dismissed of an afternoon, to stretch
himself on the rich bed of clover, bordering the little brook that
whimpered past his school-house, and there con over old Mather's direful tales, until the gathering dusk of evening made the
printed page a mere mist before his eyes. Then, as he wended his
way, by swamp and stream and awful woodland, to the farm-
house where he happened to be quartered, every sound of nature,
at that witching hour, fluttered his excited imagination: the moan
of the whip-poor-will from the hill side; the boding cry of the
tree-toad, that harbinger of storm; the dreary hooting of the
screech-owl; or the sudden rustling in the thicket, of birds frightened from their roost. The fire-flies, too, which sparkled most
vividly in the darkest places, now and then startled him, as one of
uncommon brightness would stream across his path; and if, by
chance, a huge blockhead of a beetle came winging his blundering
flight against him, the poor varlet was ready to give up the ghost,
with the idea that he was struck with a witch's token. His only
resource on such occasions, either to drown thought, or drive
away evil spirits, was to sing psalm tunes;—and the good people of
Sleepy Hollow, as they sat by their doors of an evening, were
often filled with awe, at hearing his nasal melody, "in linked

sweetness long drawn out," floating from the distant hill, or along the dusky road.

Another of his sources of fearful pleasure was, to pass long winter evenings with the old Dutch wives, as they sat spinning by the fire, with a row of apples roasting and sputtering along the hearth, and listen to their marvellous tales of ghosts and goblins, and haunted fields and haunted brooks, and haunted bridges and haunted houses, and particularly of the headless horseman, or galloping Hessian of the Hollow, as they sometimes called him. He would delight them equally by his anecdotes of witchcraft, and of the direful omens and portentous sights and sounds in the air, which prevailed in the earlier times of Connecticut; and would frighten them wofully with speculations upon comets and shooting stars, and with the alarming fact that the world did absolutely turn round, and that they were half the time topsy-turvy!

But if there was a pleasure in all this, while snugly cuddling in the chimney corner of a chamber that was all of a ruddy glow from the crackling wood fire, and where, of course, no spectre dare to show its face, it was dearly purchased by the terrors of his subsequent walk homewards. What fearful shapes and shadows beset his path, amidst the dim and ghostly glare of a snowy night!—With what wistful look did he eye every trembling ray of light streaming across the waste fields from some distant window!—How often was he appalled by some shrub covered with snow, which like sheeted spectre beset his very path!—How often did he shrink with curdling awe at the sound of his own steps on the frosty crust beneath his feet; and dread to look over his shoulder, lest he should behold some uncouth being tramping close behind him!—and how often was he thrown into complete dismay by some rushing blast, howling among the trees, in the idea that it was the galloping Hessian on one of his nightly scourings.

All these, however, were mere terrors of the night, phantoms of the mind, that walk in darkness; and though he had seen many spectres in his time, and been more than once beset by Satan in diverse shapes, in his lonely perambulations, yet day-light put an end to all these evils; and he would have passed a pleasant life of it, in despite of the Devil and all his works, if his path had not been crossed by a being that causes more perplexity to mortal man, than ghosts, goblins, and the whole race of witches put together, and that was—a woman.

Among the musical disciples who assembled, one evening in each week, to receive his instructions in psalmody, was Katrina Van Tassel, the daughter and only child of a substantial Dutch farmer. She was a blooming lass of fresh eighteen; plump as a partridge; ripe and melting and rosy cheeked as one of her father's peaches, and universally famed, not merely for her beauty, but her vast expectations. She was withal a little of a coquette, as might be perceived even in her dress, which was a mixture of ancient and modern fashions, as most suited to set off her charms. She wore the ornaments of pure yellow gold, which her great-great-grand-mother had brought over from Saardam; the tempting stomacher of the olden time, and withal a provokingly short petticoat, to display the prettiest foot and ankle in the country round.

Ichabod Crane had a soft and foolish heart toward the sex; and it is not to be wondered at, that so tempting a morsel soon found favour in his eyes, more especially after he had visited her in her paternal mansion. Old Baltus Van Tassel was a perfect picture of a thriving, contented, liberal-hearted farmer. He seldom, it is true, sent either his eyes or his thoughts beyond the boundaries of his own farm; but within those every thing was snug, happy, and well-conditioned. He was satisfied with his wealth, but not proud of it, and piqued himself upon the hearty abundance, rather than the style in which he lived. His strong hold was situated on the banks of the Hudson, in one of those green, sheltered, fertile nooks, into which the Dutch farmers are so fond of nestling. A great elm tree spread its broad branches over it, at the foot of which bubbled up a spring of the softest and sweetest water, in a little kind of well, formed of a barrel, and then stole sparkling away through the grass, to a neighbouring brook, that babbled along among elders and dwarf willows. Hard by the farm-house was a vast barn, that might have served for a church, every window and crevice of which seemed bursting forth with the treasures of the farm; the flail was busily resounding within it; swallows and martins skimmed twittering about the eaves, and rows of pigeons, some with one eye turned up, as if watching the weather, some with their heads under their wings, or buried in their bosoms, and others, swelling, and cooing, and bowing about their dames, were enjoying the sunshine on the roof. Sleek unwieldy porkers were grunting in the repose and abundance of their pens, from whence sallied forth, now and then, troops of sucking pigs, as if to snuff the air. A stately squadron of snowy geese were riding in an adjoining pond, convoying whole fleets of ducks; regiments of turkeys were gobbling about the farm-yard, and guinea fowls fretting like ill-tempered housewives, with their peevish discontented cry. Before the barn door strutted the gallant cock, that pattern of a husband, a warrior, and a fine gentleman, clapping his burnished wings, and crowing in the pride and gladness of his heart–sometimes tearing up the earth with his feet, and then generously calling his ever-hungry family of wives and children to enjoy the rich morsel he had discovered.

The pedagogue's mouth watered, as he looked upon this sumptuous promise of luxurious winter fare. In his devouring mind's eye, he pictured to himself every roasting pig running about with a pudding in its belly, and an apple in its mouth; the pigeons were snugly put to bed in a comfortable pie, and tucked in with a coverlet of crust; the geese were swimming in their own gravy; and the ducks pairing cosily in dishes, like snug married couples, with a decent competency of onion sauce; in the porkers he saw carved out the future sleek side of bacon, and juicy relishing ham; not a turkey, but he beheld daintily trussed up, with its gizzard under its wing, and, peradventure, a necklace of savoury sausages; and even bright chanticleer himself lay sprawling on his back, in a side dish, with uplifted claws, as if craving that quarter, which his chivalrous spirit disdained to ask while living.

As the enraptured Ichabod fancied all this, and as he rolled his great green eyes over the fat meadow lands, the rich fields of wheat, of rye, of buckwheat, and Indian corn, and the orchards burthened with ruddy fruit, which surrounded the warm tenement of Van Tassel, his heart yearned after the damsel who was to inherit these domains, and his imagination expanded with the

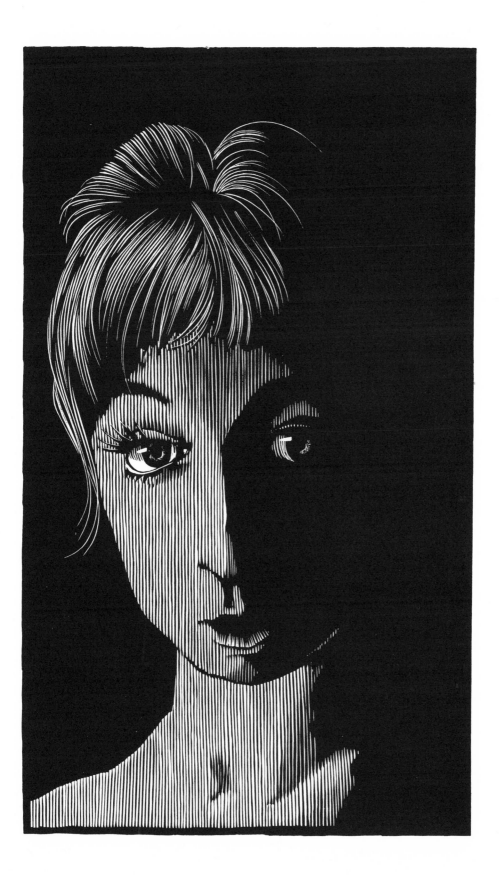

idea, how they might be readily turned into cash, and the money 33 invested in immense tracts of wild land, and shingle palaces in the wilderness. Nay, his busy fancy already put him in possession of his hopes, and presented to him the blooming Katrina, with a whole family of children, mounted on the top of a waggon loaded with household trumpery, with pots and kettles dangling beneath; and he beheld himself bestriding a pacing mare, with a colt at her heels, setting out for Kentucky, Tennessee, or the Lord knows where!

When he entered the house, the conquest of his heart was complete. It was one of those spacious farm-houses, with high-ridged, but lowly-sloping roofs, built in the style handed down from the first Dutch settlers. The low, projecting eaves formed a piazza along the front, capable of being closed up in bad weather. Under this were hung flails, harness, various utensils of husbandry, and nets for fishing in the neighbouring river. Benches were built along the sides for summer use; and a great spinning wheel at one end, and a churn at the other, showed the various uses to which this important porch might be devoted. From this piazza the wondering Ichabod entered the hall, which formed the centre of the mansion, and the place of usual residence. Here, rows of resplendent pewter, ranged on a long dresser, dazzled his eyes. In one corner stood a huge bag of wool ready to be spun; in another a quantity of linsey-woolsey just from the loom; ears of Indian corn, and strings of dried apples and peaches, hung in gay festoons along the walls, mingled with the gaud of red peppers; and a door left ajar, gave him a peep into the best parlour, where the claw-footed chairs, and dark mahogany tables, shone like mirrors; andirons, with their accompanying shovel and tongs, glistened from their covert of asparagus tops; mock oranges and conch shells decorated the mantlepiece; strings of various coloured birds' eggs were suspended above it; a great ostrich egg was hung from the centre of the room; and a corner cupboard, knowingly left open, displayed immense treasures of old silver and well-mended china.

From the moment Ichabod laid his eyes upon these regions of delight, the peace of his mind was at an end, and his only study was how to gain the affections of the peerless daughter of Van Tassel. In this enterprize, however, he had more real difficulties than generally fell to the lot of a knight-errant of yore, who seldom had any thing but giants, enchanters, fiery dragons, and such like easily conquered adversaries, to contend with; and had to make his way merely through gates of iron and brass, and walls of adamant, to the castle keep, where the lady of his heart was confined; all which he achieved as easily as a man would carve his way to the centre of a Christmas pie, and then the lady gave him her hand as a matter of course. Ichabod, on the contrary, had to win his way to the heart of a country coquette, beset with a labyrinth of whims and caprices, which were for ever presenting new difficulties and impediments, and he had to encounter a host of fearful adversaries of real flesh and blood, the numerous rustic admirers, who beset every portal to her heart, keeping a watchful and angry eye upon each other, but ready to fly out in the common cause against any new competitor.

Among these, the most formidable was a burley, roaring, roystering blade, of the name of Abraham, or, according to the Dutch abbreviation, Brom Van Brunt, the hero of the country round, which rung with his feats of strength and hardihood. He was broad shouldered and double jointed, with short curly black hair, and a bluff, but not unpleasant countenance, having a mingled air of fun and arrogance. From his Herculean frame and great powers of limb, he had received the nick-name of BROM BONES, by which he was universally known. He was famed for great knowledge and skill in horsemanship, being as dexterous on horseback as a Tartar. He was foremost at all races and cock-fights, and with the ascendancy which bodily strength always acquires in rustic life, was the umpire in all disputes, setting his hat on one side, and giving his decisions with an air and tone that admitted of no gainsay or appeal. He was always ready for either a fight or a frolick; had more mischief than ill-will in his composition; and with all his overbearing roughness, there was a strong dash of waggish good humour at bottom. He had three or four boon companions of his own stamp, who regarded him as their model, and at the head of whom he scoured the country, attending every

scene of feud or merriment for miles round. In cold weather he was distinguished by a fur cap, surmounted with a flaunting fox's tail, and when the folks at a country gathering descried this well-known crest at a distance, whisking about among a squad of hard riders, they always stood by for a squall. Sometimes his crew would be heard dashing along past the farm-houses at midnight, with whoop and halloo, like a troop of Don Cossacks, and the old dames, startled out of their sleep, would listen for a moment till the hurry scurry had clattered by, and then exclaim, "aye, there goes Brom Bones and his gang!" The neighbours looked upon him with a mixture of awe, admiration, and good-will; and when any mad-cap prank, or rustic brawl occurred in the vicinity, always shook their heads, and warranted Brom Bones was at the bottom of it.

This rantipole hero had for some time singled out the blooming Katrina for the object of his uncouth gallantries, and though his amorous toyings were something like the gentle caresses and endearments of a bear, yet it was whispered that she did not altogether discourage his hopes. Certain it is, his advances were signals for rival candidates to retire, who felt no inclination to cross a lion in his amours; insomuch, that when his horse was seen tied to Van Tassel's paling, of a Sunday night, (a sure sign that his master was courting, or, as it is termed, "sparking," within,) all other suitors passed by in despair, and carried the war into other quarters.

Such was the formidable rival with whom Ichabod Crane had to contend, and, considering all things, a stouter man than he would have shrunk from the competition, and a wiser man would have despaired. He had, however, a happy mixture of pliability and perseverance in his nature; he was in form and spirit like a supple jack–yielding, but tough; though he bent, he never broke; and though he bowed beneath the slightest pressure, yet, the moment it was away–jerk!–he was as erect, and carried his head as high as ever.

To have taken the field openly against his rival, would have been madness; for he was not a man to be thwarted in his amours, any more than that stormy lover, Achilles. Ichabod, therefore, made his advances in a quiet and gently-insinuating manner. Under cover of his character of singing master, he made frequent visits at the farm-house; not that he had any thing to apprehend from the meddlesome interference of parents, which is so often a stumbling block in the path of lovers. Balt Van Tassel was an easy indulgent soul; he loved his daughter better even than his pipe, and like a reasonable man, and an excellent father, let her have her way in every thing. His notable little wife too, had enough to do to attend to her housekeeping and manage the poultry, for, as she sagely observed, ducks and geese are foolish things, and must be looked after, but girls can take care of themselves. Thus, while the busy dame bustled about the house, or plied her spinning wheel at one end of the piazza, honest Balt would sit smoking his evening pipe at the other, watching the achievements of a little wooden warrior, who, armed with a sword in each hand, was most valiantly fighting the wind on the pinnacle of the barn. In the mean time, Ichabod would carry on his suit with the daughter by the side of the spring under the great elm, or sauntering along in the twilight, that hour so favourable to the lover's eloquence.

I profess not to know how women's hearts are wooed and won. To me they have always been matters of riddle and admiration. Some seem to have but one vulnerable point, or door of access; while others have a thousand avenues, and may be captured a thousand different ways. It is a great triumph of skill to gain the former, but a still greater proof of generalship to maintain possession of the latter, for a man must battle for his fortress at every door and window. He that wins a thousand common hearts, is therefore entitled to some renown; but he who keeps undisputed sway over the heart of a coquette, is indeed a hero. Certain it is, this was not the case with the redoubtable Brom Bones; and from the moment Ichabod Crane made his advances, the interests of the former evidently declined; his horse was no longer seen tied at the palings on Sunday nights, and a deadly feud gradually arose between him and the preceptor of Sleepy Hollow.

Brom, who had a degree of rough chivalry in his nature, would fain have carried matters to open warfare, and settled their pretensions to the lady, according to the mode of those most concise

and simple reasoners, the knights-errant of yore—by single com-
bat; but Ichabod was too conscious of the superior might of his
adversary to enter the lists against him; he had overheard the
boast of Bones, that he would "double the schoolmaster up, and
put him on a shelf;" and he was too wary to give him an opportu-
nity. There was something extremely provoking in this obsti-
nately pacific system; it left Brom no alternative but to draw upon
the funds of rustic waggery in his disposition, and play off boorish
practical jokes upon his rival. Ichabod became the object of whimsical persecution to Bones, and his gang of rough riders. They
harried his hitherto peaceful domains; smoked out his singing
school, by stopping up the chimney; broke into the school-house
at night, in spite of its formidable fastenings of withe and window
stakes, and turned every thing topsy-turvy, so that the poor
schoolmaster began to think all the witches in the country held
their meetings there. But what was still more annoying, Brom
took all opportunities of turning him into ridicule in presence of
his mistress, and had a scoundrel dog, whom he taught to whine
in the most ludicrous manner, and introduced as a rival of Ichabod's, to instruct her in psalmody.

In this way, matters went on for some time, without producing
any material effect on the relative situations of the contending
powers. On a fine autumnal afternoon, Ichabod, in pensive mood,
sat enthroned on the lofty stool from whence he usually watched
all the concerns of his little literary realm. In his hand he swayed a
ferule, that sceptre of despotic power; the birch of justice reposed
on three nails, behind the throne, a constant terror to evil doers;
while on the desk before him might be seen sundry contraband
articles and prohibited weapons, detected upon the persons of
idle urchins, such as half-munched apples, popguns, whirligigs,
fly-cages, and whole legions of rampant little paper game cocks.
Apparently there had been some appalling act of justice recently
inflicted, for his scholars were all busily intent upon their books,
or slyly whispering behind them with one eye kept upon the
master; and a kind of buzzing stillness reigned throughout the
school-room. It was suddenly interrupted by the appearance of a
negro in tow-cloth jacket and trowsers, a round crowned frag-

ment of a hat, like the cap of Mercury, and mounted on the back of a ragged, wild, half-broken colt, which he managed with a rope by way of halter. He came clattering up to the school-door with an invitation to Ichabod to attend a merry-making, or "quilting frolick," to be held that evening at Mynheer Van Tassel's, and having delivered his message with that air of importance, and effort at fine language, which a negro is apt to display on petty embassies of the kind, he dashed over the brook, and was seen scampering away up the hollow, full of the importance and hurry of his mission.

All was now bustle and hubbub in the late quiet school room. The scholars were hurried through their lessons, without stopping at trifles; those who were nimble, skipped over half with impunity, and those who were tardy, had a smart application now and then in the rear, to quicken their speed, or help them over a tall word. Books were flung aside, without being put away on the shelves; inkstands were overturned, benches thrown down, and the whole school turned loose an hour before the usual time; bursting forth like a legion of young imps, yelping and racketting about the green in joy at their early emancipation.

The gallant Ichabod now spent at least an extra half hour at his toilet, brushing and furbishing up his best, and indeed only suit of rusty black, and arranging his looks by a bit of broken looking glass, that hung up in the school house. That he might make his appearance before his mistress in the true style of a cavalier, he borrowed a horse from the farmer with whom he was domiciliated, a choleric old Dutchman, of the name of Hans Van Ripper, and thus gallantly mounted, issued forth like a knight-errant in quest of adventures. But it is meet I should, in the true spirit of romantic story, give some account of the looks and equipments of my hero and his steed. The animal he bestrode was a broken-down plough horse, that had outlived almost every thing but his viciousness. He was gaunt and shagged, with a ewe neck and hammer head; his rusty mane and tail were tangled and knotted with burrs; one eye had lost its pupil, and was glaring and spectral, but the other had the gleam of a genuine devil in it. Still he must have had fire and mettle in his day, if we may judge from his name,

which was Gunpowder. He had, in fact, been a favourite steed of
his master's, the choleric Van Ripper, who was a furious rider,
and had infused, very probably, some of his own spirit into the
animal, for, old and broken-down as he looked, there was more
lurking deviltry in him than in any young filly in the country.

Ichabod was a suitable figure for such a steed. He rode with
short stirrups, which brought his knees nearly up to the pommel
of the saddle; his sharp elbows stuck out like grasshoppers'; he
carried his whip perpendicularly in his hand, like a sceptre, and as
the horse jogged on, the motion of his arms was not unlike the
flapping of a pair of wings. A small wool hat rested on the top of
his nose, for so his scanty strip of forehead might be called, and
the skirts of his black coat fluttered out almost to the horse's tail.
Such was the appearance of Ichabod and his steed, as they sham-
bled out of the gate of Hans Van Ripper, and it was altogether
such an apparition as is seldom to be met with in broad day light.

It was, as I have said, a fine autumnal day, the sky was clear and
serene, and nature wore that rich and golden livery which we
always associate with the idea of abundance. The forests had put
on their sober brown and yellow, while some trees of the tenderer
kind had been nipped by the frosts into brilliant dyes of orange,
purple, and scarlet. Streaming files of wild ducks began to make
their appearance high in the air; the bark of the squirrel might be
heard from the groves of beech and hickory nuts, and the pensive
whistle of the quail at intervals from the neighbouring stubble
field.

The small birds were taking their farewell banquets. In the
fullness of their revelry, they fluttered, chirping and frolicking,
from bush to bush, and tree to tree, capricious from the very
profusion and variety around them. There was the honest cock-
robin, the favourite game of stripling sportsmen, with its loud
querulous note; and the twittering blackbirds flying in sable
clouds; and the golden winged woodpecker, with his crimson
crest, his broad black gorget, and splendid plumage; and the cedar
bird, with its red tipt wings and yellow tipt tail, and its little
monteiro cap of feathers; and the blue jay, that noisy coxcomb, in
his gay light blue coat and white under clothes, screaming and

chattering, nodding, and bobbing, and bowing, and pretending to be on good terms with every songster of the grove.

As Ichabod jogged slowly on his way, his eye, ever open to every symptom of culinary abundance, ranged with delight over the treasures of jolly autumn. On all sides he beheld vast store of apples, some hanging in oppressive opulence on the trees, some gathered into baskets and barrels for the market, others heaped up in rich piles for the cider-press. Further on he beheld great fields of Indian corn, with its golden ears peeping from their leafy coverts, and holding out the promise of cakes and hasty pudding; and the yellow pumpkins lying beneath them, turning up their fair round bellies to the sun, and giving ample prospects of the most luxurious of pies; and anon he passed the fragrant buckwheat fields, breathing the odour of the bee-hive, and as he beheld them, soft anticipations stole over his mind of dainty slap-jacks, well buttered, and garnished with honey or treacle, by the delicate little dimpled hand of Katrina Van Tassel.

Thus feeding his mind with many sweet thoughts and "sugared suppositions," he journeyed along the sides of a range of hills which look out upon some of the goodliest scenes of the mighty Hudson. The sun gradually wheeled his broad disk down into the west. The wide bosom of the Tappaan Zee lay motionless and glassy, excepting that here and there a gentle undulation waved and prolonged the blue shadow of the distant mountain: a few amber clouds floated in the sky, without a breath of air to move them. The horizon was of a fine golden tint, changing gradually into a pure apple green, and from that into a deep blue of the mid-heaven. A slanting ray lingered on the woody crests of the precipices that overhung some parts of the river, giving greater depth to the dark gray and purple of their rocky sides. A sloop was loitering in the distance, dropping slowly down with the tide, her sail hanging uselessly against the mast, and as the reflection of the sky gleamed along the still water, it seemed as if the vessel was suspended in the air.

It was toward evening that Ichabod arrived at the castle of the Heer Van Tassel, which he found thronged with the pride and flower of the adjacent country. Old farmers, a spare leathern-faced race, in homespun coats and small-clothes, blue stockings, huge shoes, and magnificent pewter buckles. Their brisk withered little dames in close crimped caps, long waisted short gowns, home-spun petticoats, with scissors and pincushions, and gay calico pockets, hanging on the outside. Buxom lasses, almost as anti-quated as their mothers, excepting where a straw hat, a fine rib-band, or perhaps a white frock, gave symptoms of city innova-tions. The sons, in short square-skirted coats, with rows of stu-pendous brass buttons, and their hair generally queued in the fashion of the times, especially if they could procure an eelskin for the purpose, it being esteemed throughout the country as a potent nourisher and strengthener of the hair.

Brom Bones, however, was the hero of the scene, having come to the gathering on his favourite steed Daredevil, a creature, like himself, full of mettle and mischief, and which no one but himself could manage. He was in fact noted for preferring vicious ani-mals, given to all kinds of tricks, which kept the rider in constant risk of his neck, and held a tractable well-broken horse as unwor-thy a lad of spirit.

Fain would I pause to dwell upon the world of charms that burst upon the enraptured gaze of my hero, as he entered the state parlour of Van Tassel's mansion. Not those of the bevy of buxom lasses, with their luxurious display of red and white: but the ample charms of a genuine Dutch country tea table, in the sumptuous time of autumn. Such heaped up platters of cakes of various and almost indescribable kinds, known only to experienced Dutch housewives. There was the doughty dough-nut, the tenderer oly koek, and the crisp and crumbling cruller; sweet cakes and short cakes, ginger cakes and honey cakes, and the whole family of cakes. And then there were apple pies and peach pies and pumpkin pies; not to mention slices of ham and smoked beef, together with broiled shad and roasted chickens; besides delectable dishes of preserved plums, and peaches, and pears, and quinces; with bowls of milk and cream, all mingled higgledy-piggledy, pretty much as I have enumerated them, with the motherly tea-pot sending up its clouds of vapour from the midst–Heaven bless the mark! I want breath and time to discuss this banquet as it deserves, and am too eager to get on with my story. Happily, Ichabod Crane was not in so great a hurry as his historian, but did ample justice to every dainty.

He was a kind and thankful toad, whose heart dilated in proportion as his skin was filled with good cheer, and whose spirits rose with eating, as some men's do with drink. He could not help, too, rolling his large eyes round him as he ate, and chuckling with the possibility that he might one day be lord of all this scene of almost unimaginable luxury and splendour. Then, he thought, how soon he'd turn his back upon the old school house; snap his fingers in the face of Hans Van Ripper, and every other niggardly patron, and kick any itinerant pedagogue out of doors that dared to call him comrade!

Old Baltus Van Tassel moved about among his guests with a face dilated with content and good humour, round and jolly as the harvest moon. His hospitable attentions were brief, but expressive, being confined to a shake of the hand, a slap on the shoulder, a loud laugh, and a pressing invitation to "reach to, and help themselves."

And now the sound of the music from the common room or hall, summoned to the dance. The musician was an old grey-headed negro, who had been the itinerant orchestra of the neighbourhood for more than half a century. His instrument was as old and battered as himself. The greater part of the time he scraped away on two or three strings, accompanying every movement of the bow with a motion of the head; bowing almost to the ground, and stamping with his foot whenever a fresh couple were to start.

Ichabod prided himself upon his dancing as much as upon his vocal powers. Not a limb, not a fibre about him was idle, and to have seen his loosely hung frame in full motion, and clattering about the room, you would have thought Saint Vitus himself, that blessed patron of the dance, was figuring before you in person. He was the admiration of all the negroes, who, having gathered, of all ages and sizes, from the farm and the neighbourhood, stood forming a pyramid of shining black faces at every door and window, gazing with delight at the scene, rolling their white eye balls, and showing grinning rows of ivory from ear to ear. How

could the flogger of urchins be otherwise than animated and joy-
ous; the lady of his heart was his partner in the dance; she smiled graciously in reply to all his amorous oglings, while Brom Bones, sorely smitten with love and jealousy, sat brooding by himself in one corner.

When the dance was at an end, Ichabod was attracted to a knot of the sager folks, who, with old Van Tassel, sat smoking at one end of the piazza, gossiping over former times, and drawling out long stories about the war.

This neighbourhood, at the time of which I am speaking, was one of those highly favoured places which abound with chronicle and great men. The British and American line had run near it during the war; it had, therefore, been the scene of marauding, and been infested with refugees, cow boys, and all kind of border chivalry. Just sufficient time had elapsed to enable each story teller to dress up his tale with a little becoming fiction, and in the indistinctness of his recollection, to make himself the hero of every exploit.

There was the story of Doffue Martling, a large, blue-bearded Dutchman, who had nearly taken a British frigate with an old iron nine-pounder from a mud breastwork, only that his gun burst at the sixth discharge. And there was an old gentleman who shall be nameless, being too rich a mynheer to be lightly mentioned, who in the battle of Whiteplains, being an excellent master of defence, parried a musket ball with a small sword, insomuch that he abso-lutely felt it whiz round the blade, and glance off at the hilt: in proof of which, he was ready at any time to show the sword, with the hilt a little bent. There were several more who had been equally great in the field, not one of whom but was persuaded that he had a considerable hand in bringing the war to a happy termi-nation.

But all these were nothing to the tales of ghosts and apparitions that succeeded. The neighbourhood is rich in legendary treasures of the kind. Local tales and superstitions thrive best in these shel-tered, long settled retreats; but they are trampled under foot, by the shifting throng that forms the population of most of our country places. Besides, there is not encouragement for ghosts in the generality of our villages, for they have scarce had time to take their first nap, and turn themselves in their graves, before their surviving friends have travelled away from the neighbourhood, so that when they turn out of a night to walk the rounds, they have no acquaintance left to call upon. This is perhaps the reason why we so seldom hear of ghosts excepting in our long-established Dutch communities.

The immediate cause, however, of the prevalence of supernatural stories in these parts, was doubtless owing to the vicinity of Sleepy Hollow. There was a contagion in the very air that blew from that haunted region; it breathed forth an atmosphere of dreams and fancies infecting all the land. Several of the Sleepy Hollow people were present at Van Tassel's, and, as usual, were doling out their wild and wonderful legends. Many dismal tales were told about funeral trains, and mournful cries and wailings heard and seen about the great tree where the unfortunate Major André was taken, and which stood in the neighbourhood. Some mention was made also of the woman in white, that haunted the dark glen at Raven Rock, and was often heard to shriek on winter nights before a storm, having perished there in the snow. The chief part of the stories, however, turned upon the favourite spectre of Sleepy Hollow, the headless horseman, who had been heard several times of late, patroling the country; and it was said, tethered his horse nightly among the graves in the church-yard.

The sequestered situation of this church seems always to have made it a favourite haunt of troubled spirits. It stands on a knoll, surrounded by locust trees and lofty elms, from among which its decent, whitewashed walls shine modestly forth, like Christian purity, beaming through the shades of retirement. A gentle slope descends from it to a silver sheet of water, bordered by high trees, between which, peeps may be caught at the blue hills of the Hudson. To look upon its grass-grown yard, where the sunbeams seem to sleep so quietly, one would think that here at least the dead might rest in peace. On one side of the church extends a wide woody dell, along which raves a large brook among broken rocks and trunks of fallen trees. Over a deep black part of the stream, not far from the church, was formerly thrown a wooden bridge; the

road that led to it, and the bridge itself, were thickly shaded by
overhanging trees, which cast a gloom about it, even in the day
time; but occasioned a fearful darkness at night. Such was one of
the favourite haunts of the headless horseman, and the place
where he was most frequently encountered. The tale was told of
old Brouwer, a most heretical disbeliever in ghosts, that he met
the horseman returning from his foray into Sleepy Hollow, and
was obliged to get up behind him; that they gallopped over bush
and brake, over hill and swamp, until they reached the bridge,
when the horseman suddenly turned into a skeleton, threw old
Brouwer into the brook, and sprang away over the tree-tops with
a clap of thunder.

This story was immediately matched by a thrice marvellous
adventure of Brom Bones, who made light of the gallopping
Hessian as an errant jockey. He affirmed, that on returning one
night from the neighbouring village of Sing-Sing, he had been
overtaken by this midnight trooper; that he had offered to race
with him for a bowl of punch, and would have won it too, for
Daredevil beat the goblin horse all hollow, but just as they came to
the church bridge, the Hessian bolted, and vanished in a flash of
fire.

All these tales, told in that drowsy under tone with which men
talk in the dark, the countenances of the listeners only now and
then receiving a casual gleam from the glare of a pipe, sunk deep in
the mind of Ichabod. He repaid them in kind with large extracts
from his invaluable author, Cotton Mather, and added many very
marvellous events that had taken place in his native state of Connecticut, and fearful sights which he had seen in his nightly walks
about Sleepy Hollow.

The revel now gradually broke up. The old farmers gathered
together their families in their wagons, and were heard for some
time rattling along the hollow roads, and over the distant hills.
Some of the damsels, mounted on pillions behind their favourite
swains, and their light-hearted laughter mingling with the clatter
of hoofs, echoed along the silent woodlands, sounding fainter and
fainter until they gradually died away–and the late scene of noise
and frolick was all silent and deserted. Ichabod only lingered

behind, according to the custom of country lovers, to have a tête-a-tête with the heiress; fully convinced that he was now on the high road to success. What passed at this interview I will not pretend to say, for in fact I do not know. Something, however, I fear me, must have gone wrong, for he certainly sallied forth, after no very great interval, with an air quite desolate and chopfallen–Oh these women! these women! Could that girl have been playing off any of her coquettish tricks?–Was her encouragement of the poor pedagogue all a mere sham to secure her conquest of his rival?–Heaven only knows, not I!–Let it suffice to say, Ichabod stole forth with the air of one who had been sacking a hen roost, rather than a fair lady's heart. Without looking to the right or left to notice the scene of rural wealth, on which he had so often gloated, he went straight to the stable, and with several hearty cuffs and kicks, roused his steed most uncourteously from the comfortable quarters in which he was soundly sleeping, dreaming of mountains of corn and oats, and whole valleys of timothy and clover.

It was the very witching time of night that Ichabod, heavy-hearted and bedrooped, pursued his travel homewards, along the sides of the lofty hills which rise above Tarry Town, and which he had traversed so cheerily in the afternoon. The hour was as dismal as himself. Far below him the Tappaan Zee spread its dusky and indistinct waste of waters, with here and there the tall mast of a sloop, riding quietly at anchor under the land. In the dead hush of midnight, he could even hear the barking of the watch-dog from the opposite shore of the Hudson; but it was so vague and faint as only to give an idea of his distance from this faithful companion of man. Now and then, too, the long-drawn crowing of a cock, accidentally awakened, would sound far, far off, from some farm house away among the hills–but it was like a dreaming sound in his ear. No signs of life occurred near him, but occasionally the melancholy chirp of a cricket, or perhaps the guttural twang of a bull frog, from a neighbouring marsh, as if sleeping uncomfortably, and turning suddenly in his bed.

All the stories of ghosts and goblins that Ichabod had heard in the afternoon, now came crowding upon his recollection. The

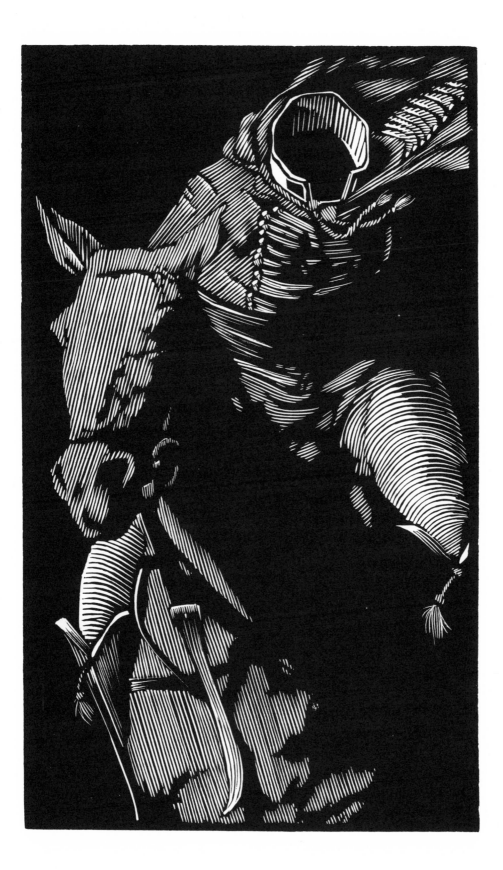

night grew darker and darker; the stars seemed to sink deeper in the sky, and driving clouds occasionally hid them from his sight. He had never felt so lonely and dismal. He was, moreover, approaching the very place where many of the scenes of the ghost stories had been laid. In the centre of the road stood an enormous tulip tree, which towered like a giant above all the other trees of the neighbourhood, and formed a kind of land-mark. Its limbs were vast, gnarled, and fantastic, twisting down almost to the earth, and rising again into the air, and they would have formed trunks for ordinary trees. It was connected with the tragical story of the unfortunate André, who had been taken prisoner hard by it, and it was universally known by the name of Major André's tree. The common people regarded it with a mixture of respect and superstition, partly out of sympathy for the memory of its ill-starred namesake, and partly from the tales, strange sights, and doleful lamentations, told concerning it.

As Ichabod approached this fearful tree, he began to whistle; he thought his whistle was answered: it was but a blast sweeping sharply through the dry branches. As he approached a little nearer, he thought he saw something white, hanging in the midst of the tree: he paused and ceased whistling; but on looking more narrowly, perceived that it was a place where the tree had been scathed by lightning, and the white wood laid bare. Suddenly he heard a groan–his teeth chattered, and his knees smote against the saddle: it was but the rubbing of one huge bough upon another, as they were swayed about by the breeze. He passed the tree in safety, but new perils lay still before him.

About two hundred yards from the tree, a small brook crossed the road, and ran into a marshy and thickly wooded glen, known by the name of Wiley's Swamp. A few rough logs, laid side by side, served for a bridge over this stream. On that side of the road where the brook entered the wood, a group of oaks and chestnuts, matted thick with wild grape vines, threw a cavernous gloom over it. To pass this bridge, was the severest trial. It was at this identical spot that the unfortunate André was captured, and under the covert of those chestnuts and vines were the sturdy yeomen concealed who surprised him. This has ever since been considered a haunted stream, and fearful are the feelings of the schoolboy who has to pass it alone after dark.

As he approached the stream, his heart began to thump; he, however, summoned up all his resolution, gave his horse half a score of kicks in the ribs, and attempted to dash briskly across the bridge; but instead of starting forward, the perverse old animal made a lateral movement, and ran broadside against the fence. Ichabod, whose fears increased with the delay, jerked the reins on the other side, and kicked lustily with the contrary foot: it was all in vain; his steed started, it is true, but it was only to plunge to the opposite side of the road into a thicket of brambles and alder bushes. The schoolmaster now bestowed both whip and heel upon the starvelling ribs of old Gunpowder, who dashed forward, snuffling and snorting, but came to a stand just by the bridge with a suddenness that had nearly sent his rider sprawling over his head. Just at this moment a plashy tramp by the side of the bridge caught the sensitive ear of Ichabod. In the dark shadow of the grove, on the margin of the brook, he beheld something huge, misshapen, black and towering. It stirred not, but seemed gathered up in the gloom, like some gigantic monster ready to spring upon the traveller.

The hair of the affrighted pedagogue rose upon his head with terror. What was to be done? To turn and fly was now too late; and besides, what chance was there of escaping ghost or goblin, if such it was, which can ride upon the wings of the wind? Summoning up, therefore, a show of courage, he demanded in stammering accents–"who are you?" He received no reply. He repeated his demand in a still more agitated voice.–Still there was no answer. Once more he cudgelled the sides of the inflexible Gunpowder, and shutting his eyes, broke forth with involuntary fervour into a psalm tune. Just then the shadowy object of alarm put itself in motion, and with a scramble and a bound, stood at once in the middle of the road. Though the night was dark and dismal, yet the form of the unknown might now in some degree be ascertained. He appeared to be a horseman of large dimensions, and mounted on a black horse of powerful frame. He made no offer of molestation or sociability, but kept aloof on one side of the road, jogging

along on the blind side of old Gunpowder, who had now got over his fright and waywardness.

Ichabod, who had no relish for this strange midnight companion, and bethought himself of the adventure of Brom Bones with the gallopping Hessian, now quickened his steed, in hopes of leaving him behind. The stranger, however, quickened his horse to an equal pace; Ichabod pulled up, and fell into a walk, thinking to lag behind–the other did the same. His heart began to sink within him; he endeavoured to resume his psalm tune, but his parched tongue clove to the roof of his mouth, and he could not utter a stave. There was something in the moody and dogged silence of this pertinacious companion, that was mysterious and appalling. It was soon fearfully accounted for. On mounting a rising ground, which brought the figure of his fellow traveller in relief against the sky, gigantic in height, and muffled in a cloak, Ichabod was horror-struck, on perceiving that he was headless! but his horror was still more increased, on observing, that the head, which should have rested on his shoulders, was carried before him on the pommel of the saddle! His terror rose to desperation; he rained a shower of kicks and blows upon Gunpowder, hoping, by a sudden movement, to give his companion the slip– but the spectre started full jump with him. Away, then, they dashed, through thick and thin; stones flying, and sparks flashing, at every bound. Ichabod's flimsy garments fluttered in the air, as he stretched his long lank body away over his horse's head, in the eagerness of his flight.

They had now reached the road which turns off to Sleepy Hollow; but Gunpowder, who seemed possessed with a demon, instead of keeping up it, made an opposite turn, and plunged headlong down hill to the left. This road leads through a sandy hollow shaded by trees for about a quarter of a mile, where it crosses the bridge famous in goblin story, and just beyond swells the green knoll on which stands the whitewashed church.

As yet the panic of the steed had given his unskilful rider an apparent advantage in the chace, but just as he had got half way through the hollow, the girths of the saddle gave way, and he felt it slipping from under him; he seized it by the pommel, and endeavoured to hold it firm, but in vain; and had just time to save himself by clasping old Gunpowder round the neck, when the saddle fell to the earth, and he heard it trampled under foot by his pursuer. For a moment the terror of Hans Van Ripper's wrath passed across his mind—for it was his Sunday saddle; but this was no time for petty fears: the goblin was hard on his haunches; and, unskilful rider that he was! he had much-ado to maintain his seat; sometimes slipping on one side, sometimes on another, and sometimes jolted on the high ridge of his horse's back bone, with a violence that he verily feared would cleave him asunder.

An opening in the trees now cheered him with the hopes that the Church Bridge was at hand. The wavering reflection of a silver star in the bosom of the brook told him that he was not mistaken. He saw the walls of the church dimly glaring under the trees beyond. He recollected the place where Brom Bones' ghostly competitor had disappeared. "If I can but reach that bridge," thought Ichabod, "I am safe." Just then he heard the black steed panting and blowing close behind him; he fancied he felt his hot breath. Another convulsive kick in the ribs, and old Gunpowder sprung upon the bridge; he thundered over the resounding planks; he gained the opposite side, and now Ichabod cast a look behind to see if his pursuer should vanish, according to rule, in a flash of fire and brimstone. Just then he saw the goblin rising in his stirrups, and in the very act of hurling his head at him. Ichabod endeavoured to dodge the horrible missile, but too late. It encountered his cranium with a tremendous crash—he was tumbled headlong into the dust, and Gunpowder, the black steed, and the goblin rider, passed by like a whirlwind.—

The next morning the old horse was found without his saddle, and the bridle under his feet, soberly cropping the grass at his master's gate. Ichabod did not make his appearance at breakfast— dinner-hour came, but no Ichabod. The boys assembled at the school-house, and strolled idly about the banks of the brook; but no schoolmaster. Hans Van Ripper now began to feel some uneasiness about the fate of poor Ichabod, and his saddle. An inquiry was set on foot, and after diligent investigation they came upon his traces. In one part of the road leading to the church, was found the saddle trampled in the dirt; the tracks of horses' hoofs

deeply dented in the road, and evidently at furious speed, were
traced to the bridge, beyond which, on the bank of a broad part of
the brook, where the water ran deep and black, was found the hat
of the unfortunate Ichabod, and close beside it a shattered pumpkin.

The brook was searched, but the body of the schoolmaster was
not to be discovered. Hans Van Ripper, as executor of his estate,
examined the bundle which contained all his worldly effects. They
consisted of two old shirts and a half; two stocks for the neck; a
pair of worsted stockings with holes in them; an old pair of cordu-
roy small-clothes; a book of psalm tunes full of dog's ears; a pitch
pipe out of order; a rusty razor; a small pot of bear's grease for the
hair, and a cast-iron comb. As to the books and furniture of the
schoolhouse, they belonged to the community, excepting Cotton
Mather's History of Witchcraft, a New-England Almanack, and a
book of dreams and fortune telling, in which last was a sheet of
foolscap much scribbled and blotted, by several fruitless attempts
to make a copy of verses in honour of the heiress of Van Tassel.
These magic books and the poetic scrawl were forthwith con-
signed to the flames by Hans Van Ripper, who from that time
forward determined to send his children no more to school, observing, that he never knew any good come of this same reading
and writing. Whatever money the schoolmaster possessed, and he
had received his quarter's pay but a day or two before, he must
have had about his person at the time of his disappearance.

The mysterious event caused much speculation at the church on
the following Sunday. Knots of gazers and gossips were collected
in the church-yard, at the bridge, and at the spot where the hat and
pumpkin had been found. The stories of Brouwer, of Bones, and a
whole budget of others, were called to mind; and when they had
diligently considered them all, and compared them with the
symptoms of the present case, they shook their heads, and came to
the conclusion, that Ichabod had been carried off by the gallopping Hessian. As he was a bachelor, and in nobody's debt, nobody
troubled his head any more about him; the school was removed to
a different quarter of the hollow, and another pedagogue reigned
in his stead.

It is true, an old farmer, who had been down to New-York on

52   a visit several years after, and from whom this account of the ghostly adventure was received, brought home the intelligence that Ichabod Crane was still alive; that he had left the neighbourhood partly through fear of the goblin and Hans Van Ripper, and partly in mortification at having been suddenly dismissed by the heiress; that he had changed his quarters to a distant part of the country; had kept school and studied law at the same time; had been admitted to the bar, turned politician, electioneered, written for the newspapers, and finally had been made a Justice of the Ten Pound Court. Brom Bones too, who, shortly after his rival's disappearance, conducted the blooming Katrina in triumph to the altar, was observed to look exceedingly knowing whenever the story of Ichabod was related, and always burst into a hearty laugh at the mention of the pumpkin; which led some to suspect that he knew more about the matter than he chose to tell.

The old country wives, however, who are the best judges of these matters, maintain to this day, that Ichabod was spirited away by supernatural means; and it is a favourite story often told about the neighbourhood round the winter evening fire. The bridge became more than ever an object of superstitious awe; and that may be the reason why the road has been altered of late years, so as to approach the church by the border of the millpond. The schoolhouse being deserted, soon fell to decay, and was reported to be haunted by the ghost of the unfortunate pedagogue; and the plough boy, loitering homeward of a still summer evening, has often fancied his voice at a distance, chanting a melancholy psalm tune among the tranquil solitudes of Sleepy Hollow.

POSTSCRIPT,

FOUND IN THE HANDWRITING OF
MR. KNICKERBOCKER.

The preceding Tale is given, almost in the precise words in which I heard it related at a corporation meeting of the ancient city of the Manhattoes, at which were present many of its sagest and most illustrious burghers. The narrator was a pleasant, shabby, gentlemanly old fellow, in pepper and salt clothes, with a sadly humourous face, and one whom I strongly suspected of being poor, he made such efforts to be entertaining. When his story was concluded, there was much laughter and approbation, particularly from two or three deputy aldermen, who had been asleep the greater part of the time. There was, however, one tall, dry-looking old gentleman, with beetling eyebrows, who maintained a grave and rather severe face throughout; now and then folding his arms, inclining his head, and looking down upon the floor, as if turning a doubt over in his mind. He was one of your wary men, who never laugh but upon good grounds–when they have reason and the law on their side. When the mirth of the rest of the company had subsided, and silence was restored, he leaned one arm on the elbow of his chair, and sticking the other a-kimbo, demanded, with a slight, but exceedingly sage motion of the head, and contraction of the brow, what was the moral of the story, and what it went to prove.

The story-teller, who was just putting a glass of wine to his lips, as a refreshment after his toils, paused for a moment, looked at his inquirer with an air of infinite deference, and lowering the glass

54 slowly to the table, observed, that the story was intended most logically to prove,

"That there is no situation in life but has its advantages and pleasures, provided we will but take a joke as we find it:

"That, therefore, he that runs races with goblin troopers, is likely to have rough riding of it:

"Ergo, for a country schoolmaster to be refused the hand of a Dutch heiress, is a certain step to high preferment in the state."

The cautious old gentleman knit his brows tenfold closer after this explanation, being sorely puzzled by the ratiocination of the syllogism; while methought the one in pepper and salt eyed him with something of a triumphant leer. At length he observed, that all this was very well, but still he thought the story a little on the extravagant–there were one or two points on which he had his doubts.

"Faith, sir," replied the story-teller, "as to that matter, I don't believe one half of it myself."

D.K.

NOTES ON THE PRINTS

As I approached these two texts, my mind's eye was strongly influenced by vivid childhood memories: Walt Disney's crane-like Ichabod, the horseman's terrifying ride across the covered bridge, the hurtling jack-o-lantern. There were also refugees from some barely remembered book: a crew of Dutch Dwarfs haunting deep ravines full of thunder. However, as I came to work the two tales, I found myself ill at ease with the notion of plagiarizing those early memories. My "inner critic," as Ben Shahn called it, has no truck with expected imagery. It is incumbent upon the illustrator to provoke the text, not merely to decorate.

My illustrations would not be complete without the Headless Horseman, Hendrick Hudson, Rip Van Winkle, Ichabod Crane. Other images are just as interesting to me as Hendrick Hudson's crew, yet these may not be what the average reader would expect to see. For instance, in this reading one encounters an outrageously becombed cock. The image is at first glance puzzling, but upon reflection the chauvinism of this chanticleer is an underlying theme of the story.

Most artists have favorite themes which they either point up or inject into the text. Flora, portraits, animals, and landscapes inevitably find their way into my imagery. I am more interested in face than costume, character than environment. I especially enjoyed creating characterizations of the shrewish Dame Van Winkle, the lackadaisical Rip Van Winkle, Rip junior, and grizzled old Rip. Likewise, Katrina Von Tassel, Brom Bones, Ichabod Crane, and Old Gunpowder.

In my ongoing search for the faces of characters I quite accidentally came across an 1869 photograph by Napoleon Sarony, of the actor Jo Jefferson as Rip Van Winkle. The characterization seemed so humorously apropos I could not resist using it—in fact, quoting it explicitly—for my figure of Rip Van Winkle.

Barry Moser, West Hatfield